Love & Honor

Holidays in Hallbrook

Elsie Davis

Sweet Romance Publishing

Sweet Romance Publishing

Sweetromancepublishing.com

PO Box 778

Liberty, NC 27298

This story is dedicated to all the women and men who serve/served in our military forces and the families who support/supported them.

There is an extensive list of brave men in my own family, who for generations served in the military, soldiers who sacrificed of themselves for our country. It is with honor I write this story for all of you—especially my father, Leon M. Cornell, who fought and died serving the country he loved.

I would also like to thank the American Humane and Mission K-9 organizations for their dedicated efforts to reuniting soldiers with their canine besties!!!

And many thanks to Dan Johnson for his help in getting the details right.

Put on the full armor of God,

so that you can take your stand against the devil's schemes.

Ephesians 6:11

Chapter One

♥

SIERRA COULDN'T HELP BUT notice the curiosity-filled gazes of other people in the Piggly Wiggly as she shopped for food. A young woman with a cane and a limp wasn't the norm. By now, you'd think she'd be used to the stares, but life didn't always work that way. It had been almost three months since her squad walked into a trap. A bomb had exploded, killing one soldier and wounding two others besides herself and Rhaegar, her precious canine soldier.

Three weeks ago, she'd been released from the hospital and returned home for convalescent leave. Her con leave had been issued for ninety days, with a checkup for further evaluation to determine her fate with the Army. She was a career soldier, but a desk job had never been part of her plans. But then she also hadn't planned on failure and returning home disgraced to face her father, a retired military commander.

It was a ten-second window that would keep repeating in her mind. The first sergeant typically made the decisions for the squad, but with enemy forces nearby, there hadn't been time to confer with him. She'd been in the front, Rhaegar trying to sniff out explosives. The decision had been hers, and the blame for making the wrong choice landed squarely on her shoulders.

If only I'd chosen the other path.

It was a decision she'd have to live with the rest of her life, and her leg was a painful daily reminder—lest she dare forget. Not that anyone else was blaming her. They weren't.

Well, except for her father, that is. Not that he'd voiced his opinion, but his attitude and expression said it all. Retired Colonel Winters didn't make mistakes, and he expected nothing less from those around him. Including her, whether as his daughter or as a soldier.

Sierra finished picking out a wide variety of products for her loaded shopping cart, not knowing exactly what the Jackson family would want. She was unwilling to arrive empty-handed and unannounced at her buddy's house.

In August, Tank had stopped by the hospital to see her before leaving Afghanistan and the Army. Bruce Jackson was a good soldier, and strong as an ox, which had earned him the nickname Tank. Although he claimed the decision to request a discharge had nothing to do with the bombing and everything to do with a girl back home, Sierra couldn't help but wonder. He was in her unit and was one of the men she'd failed.

She hadn't seriously considered Tank's generous offer to visit the Jackson ranch, at least, not until she'd found herself back stateside and living with her parents. They had driven her crazy, to the point she had to leave. More specifically, her dictatorial and ever-judging father had caused her to go. The man who excelled at everything Army and thought women should never take part in active military operations. Old school at its worst. Hallbrook, NH, had started to sound like a heaven-sent offer. Especially with the bonus of seeing her friend.

Sierra's leg was bothering her, a sure sign she'd been on her feet too long. She pushed her cart toward the front of the store and made a beeline for the front register with no one in line. Unfortunately, it seemed she wasn't the only one who thought it was their lucky day, her cart colliding with another shopper.

"I'm so sorry." The man's deep, gravelly voice with a quick apology kept her from saying the first thing that came to mind as the shaft of pain radiating down her leg multiplied. The military life hadn't exactly had her playing niceties in a tearoom setting for the past ten years.

"It's fine. I should have been paying closer attention." Sierra grimaced. The throbbing had increased to an eight, and she reached down to apply a massage technique to her leg. Numbering the pain level was automatic after three months of every doctor and nurse she encountered, asking the question twenty times a day.

"Go ahead, ma'am," the man said, pulling back on his cart slightly to make room for her. The guy was tall, with steel-blue eyes and jet-black hair and there was no missing his curious gaze as he glanced from where her hand rubbed her leg, to her cane, and then back at her. He was no different than everyone else.

"Why? You were clearly here first." Sierra was tired of people treating her like an invalid, and his condescending attitude rankled.

"Because it's the right thing to do, is why." He frowned, but otherwise, his expression wasn't easy to read.

"The right thing how? Or is it because you feel sorry for me because I'm crippled?" Sierra pressed for the truth. She was tired of skirting around the issue, and this lucky guy was the recipient of her pent-up anger.

"No. Yes. Maybe." He shrugged. "Mostly because you're a woman, and I was taught respect and to show common courtesy toward women. I wasn't trying to offend you." He shook his head, his expression more dumbfounded than anything else.

"Well, you did. Try living in the twenty-first century, mister. Since you were here first, go first," she ground out. Sierra was unsure whether to be more offended by the because-you're-a-woman comment or the fact he'd more or less admitted it was because she was crippled.

"Suit yourself." The man stepped forward and started to unload his groceries. Judging by the ache in her leg and her order's size, she should have taken him up on his offer. The guy looked like he was buying for an army.

The one thing Sierra hated more than anything was being mollycoddled. For any reason. It was something that had always annoyed her. It hadn't taken her long to correct the poor saps in the military who'd tried to treat her as if she were the weaker sex, but she'd never been able to break her father of the habit.

The colonel had wanted a son and gotten a daughter, something he never let her forget. But not in the way most people would expect. He'd wanted her to be all girly, insisting she wear dresses, play with dolls, have tea parties, and help her mother hostess events. Basically, all things feminine and dainty. Sierra was a failure in the kitchen. Although, to be fair, she'd messed up recipes or burnt meals to prove a point and get out of cooking. Eventually, it had worked, and her mother had ordered her out of the kitchen. *Permanently.*

Sierra had always been an adventurous child, something her father couldn't or wouldn't accept. And when she'd turned eighteen, she'd done the only thing possible to escape his overbearing ways—she'd joined the Army.

A chip off the old block.

Noah paid for his groceries, eager to leave and forget about the prickly woman in line. "Thanks, Katie. See you next time." He shot a quick smile at the cashier and headed for the door without so much as a backward glance at the customer behind him. The woman's sour attitude had been surprising given he was only trying to be nice. Clearly, she wasn't in the mood for nice or anything else for that matter.

He'd noticed her earlier walking through the produce aisle. With short, blonde hair that framed her pretty face and dark eyes, and a T-shirt that revealed an athletic figure, he'd been curious about the stranger in town. But when she walked a few steps, he'd spotted the limp and instantly gone into more of a concerned mode.

It was only natural for him considering his medical training. He couldn't have stopped trying to assess the situation any more than he could stop his seven-year-old daughter from begging to stay up late every night. Some things were out of one's control.

It had been his turn to run to the Piggly Wiggly for the weekly groceries, a chore he sorely disliked. He dealt with the public all day at the hospital, and the last thing he needed was to deal with more people. Especially women like the prickly pear he'd had the misfortune of running into. *Literally.*

Part of him understood her defensive rhetoric— the medically trained part. If she'd suffered a recent injury, there was a good chance she was still super sensitive about it. As to her femininity, his guess was that she'd been raised by a strong woman, the kind who didn't appreciate chivalry. His mother had raised him differently, but then living in a small town where everyone knew everybody, it could also be labeled respect.

He loaded the groceries in his truck and slid in the front seat, anxious to get back to the ranch and his daughter. His mother did her best, showering Kaylee with love and attention, but she sometimes spoiled her, leaving Noah to deal with her pouty attitude at the end of the evening. After Blanche divorced him, living with his mother hadn't been ideal, but moving home to the ranch was short-term and for the best. The new house would be done before Christmas, and Noah was looking forward to some personal space, something he rarely got now.

Noah backed the truck out of the parking space and headed toward the exit that led to Main Street. As he waited for traffic to clear, he noticed a blue truck behind him. Checking traffic both ways again, he pulled out onto the street.

Jackson Ranch wasn't far outside of the town limits, making it a quick drive. Three turns later, he couldn't help but notice the same blue truck behind him. A sense of curiosity and caution washed over Noah, the neighborhood-watch program kicking into gear. Few people lived out this way, and it made him wonder who was following. Once they passed the Miller place, there was nothing else except his family ranch and a dead-end after that. When the truck still followed him after the Miller's, he slowed down, trying to get a good look at the driver, but road dust obliterated the view in his rearview mirror.

Noah parked in front of the house and got out of the truck. He waited for the other vehicle to come to a stop as the driver parked next to him. The door opened, and a familiar blonde slid out of the driver's seat. *The prickly woman from the store.*

"Follow me home to offer more insults?" he asked, confused by her presence.

"You? What are you doing here?" The woman didn't seem so sure of herself now, not like she had in the store.

"I live here. Question is, what are *you* doing here?" He moved closer, determined to find out why she was stalking him, and then make her leave.

"I'm here to see a friend. Tank... *ummm*, Bruce Jackson. This is the address he gave me." Her gaze shot to the front porch and then back to him.

Figures. She was here to see his brother. It shouldn't come as a surprise, but it did. And not in a good way. His brother always had an eye for a pretty woman, and they for him. And his military image hadn't hurt his reputation, not even after he'd gotten out a couple of months ago.

"I'm Noah. Noah Jackson. Bruce's brother. You're in the right place." He nodded, reaching out to shake hands. Formalities over, he made a move toward the house. "Wait right here, and I'll get him." He didn't bother to hang around for an answer, taking the porch steps two at a time. Let Bruce figure out what to do with the woman since he obviously knew her enough to give her their address.

Noah couldn't help but wonder how well Bruce and they were acquainted. The prickly woman and his brother didn't fit together as a likely couple. And for some strange reason, he didn't want them to fit—not that he was interested—he wasn't. One marriage had been more than enough to put him off relationships.

Chapter Two

♥

SIERRA WATCHED NOAH AS he headed toward the front door. She still couldn't believe Tank's brother was the man from the Piggly Wiggly. She knew Tank had a brother, but that's where the information stopped. Her buddy hadn't been big on talking about family, and neither had she, which is why they'd hit it off so well. Or at least it had been that way until they'd gotten to know each other better. Sometimes in the dark of night, confidences were shared. But Tank had never mentioned anything about Noah, making him an enigma.

"Bruce!" he hollered, holding the screen door open. "You've got a visitor."

"What? I'm not expecting any—holy Toledo. I can't believe it." Smiling eyes and a matching grin lit Tank's face when he spotted her. "Sierra Winters. Well, I'll be dipped in dirt and hogtied."

Sierra let out the breath she'd been holding. Her friend's welcome was rock solid, and his familiar friendly voice managed to put her at ease. "Hey, Tank." She grinned, shooting an I-told-you-so smirk at Noah.

Tank practically jumped off the porch, clearing the steps quickly, and scooped her up in his arms to swing her around before setting her back down to look at her. "Why didn't you let me know you were coming?"

She fought back against the stab of pain in her leg. "I wasn't sure until I found myself crossing the New Hampshire state line, to be honest. I wasn't sure where I *was headed*, but here I am. If it's still okay with you, that is? You know, your offer and all."

"Of course, it is. I meant every word. How's the leg?"

Sierra had known he would ask, and she'd played out her answer repeatedly in her head. If she told him the truth, he'd make a fuss. She'd had enough of that from her parents. Unfortunately, Noah had witnessed one of her less-than-stellar moments, and Sierra could only hope he'd keep their encounter to himself.

"It has its good days and bad days. How have you been?" It was a safe enough question, considering the mutual understanding that prohibited in-depth discussions about the blast. Sierra could only hope he no longer suffered from the same flashbacks she did, the replay button going off at times she couldn't control. It was normal after what they'd been through, but Sierra didn't have to like it.

"I'm all right. You know how it is." He pulled her in for a hug again and then tried to pull her toward the porch.

"Hang on, Tank." Reaching back into the car, she grabbed her cane. This was the part she hated—the part where everyone's eyes filled with sympathy.

Tank glanced down at it, his lips tightening into a hard line. "Sierra? What's really going on?"

"It's fine, trust me. Just some lingering issues." She shrugged, hoping to convince him to let it go. The last thing she wanted to do was get into the gritty details of her repeated surgeries, complications, and endless doctor visits that had left her future in the military uncertain.

"If you say so. Does that mean you're out?" Sierra knew what he meant without further explanation.

"No. Ninety-day con leave. I report back by December 6th."

His eyebrows shot up. "All things considered, that's not much time given how it seems now."

"It just looks bad, but it's nothing I can't handle. Loads of PT exercises and rest. I'll be champing at the bit to return to work by then. You know me." She forced a brave smile to back up her words.

Tank nodded. "Okay, then. Come meet the family."

They headed up the steps to where three people waited on the porch. She couldn't help the slow pace or the limp, but she lifted her chin, determined not to be a coward.

"This is my mother, Laura. My brother, Noah. And his daughter, Kaylee. Everyone, this is Sierra Winters. We were stationed together in Afghanistan."

"It's nice to meet you all." Sierra offered her hand to Tank's mother first.

"Welcome to our ranch," his mother said, a genuine smile on her face as she clasped Sierra's hand.

Noah stepped forward, taking her hand in his firm grip. "We've met. Sort of. Unofficially anyway."

Tank narrowed his eyes as he glanced back and forth between them. "Oh? How's that? I thought you just arrived, Sierra?"

"I met your brother at the Piggly Wiggly when I stopped in on the way here. Which reminds me, I brought groceries. I didn't know what to get, so I picked up some basics, hoping it would help."

"You didn't have to do that. Round here, folks are always welcome. Especially friends," Tank playfully pushed against her shoulder. Not like any of the hundreds of times he'd done it before. This time he did it gently—like she was an invalid. She'd give him a pass this time. Getting knocked off her feet wasn't high on her priority list.

The little girl moved to stand next to her. "Hi, Miss Sierra. I like your name. It's pretty like you." Kaylee reached out to shake Sierra's hand, imitating the grown-ups.

"It's nice to meet you, too. And I love your name," Sierra said, smiling down at her.

Kaylee beamed, clutching a stuffed animal tightly in one hand. She looked up at Noah with adoration shining on her face, almost as if looking to him for approval. It gave Sierra pause, realizing the guy couldn't be all bad, even if they had gotten off to a rocky start.

"We don't need anything, considering I just did a full shopping run—as you know," Noah interjected. The man was still frowning, but then she couldn't blame him. She had been on the rude side, and there was no use trying to justify her actions. Her problems were her own and not his fault.

It was then that his words sank in. We...shopping... Noah lived here. In fact, they all lived here, judging by what she was hearing. This wasn't good. The plan had been to visit Tank and his mother. Not move in with the whole family. "I... *ummm...*" She glanced at Tank, unsure of what to say.

"I invited her to come and stay at the ranch. It would seem she's taking me up on my offer." Tank smiled as if it was a given and no one would care. "Noah's right, you didn't have to bring groceries— just yourself. But seeing as you've already gone to all the trouble, I'll get them out of the car and into the house. Why don't you have a seat on the porch and rest." His gaze flickered down to her leg and cane. She'd have something to say to him about that later when they were alone. Set the record straight. He, of all people, should know she wouldn't want to be babied or treated with special care.

"I think it's a lovely idea," Laura said, her kind and gracious smile welcoming.

"She can't stay here. You all seem to be forgetting the current situation," Noah spoke up, shaking his head.

Everyone turned to look at him, confusion in their expressions.

"Why not, Daddy? It would be funner to have someone else here to play with?" Kaylee asked.

"More fun, but to answer your question—we don't have the room. No one has thought this through, and she can't exactly stay in Bruce's room. I have an impressionable seven-year-old, and the other bedrooms are all taken."

Bruce coughed. "I wasn't suggesting my bedroom. When I made the invitation, I hadn't realized my big brother and niece had moved back home. Back then, I offered a guest bedroom."

Sierra didn't want to cause any problems, and she tried to set the record straight. "First off, if there's an issue with me staying, it's no big deal. I've got plenty of places I can go," she lied. "Second, I'm not Tank's girlfriend. I don't have time for such romantic nonsense."

"Not to mention, she outranks me. Did outrank me, given she's the only one still serving," Tank added with a roll of his eyes and a quick grin. "The military frowns on fraternization."

"It sounds like things have changed here. I should have called first. I'm sorry." Sierra turned and started for the stairs, prepared to leave. The last thing she wanted to do was cause trouble. Leaving was the right choice, just not an easy one because she didn't know where else to go. Back home wasn't an option. And the only thing worse than being with her parents was being alone with her nightmares.

"You'll do no such thing." Laura stepped forward to take her by the arm. "We always have room for visitors, especially a friend." Mrs. Jackson was being a gracious host and settling the disagreement between her sons like a pro. It was more than a little awkward to realize she was the reason for the dispute.

"And where do you propose she sleep? On the couch? It's not exactly comfortable or hospitable to put her in the middle of the living room," Noah chimed in. He acted like a man used to getting his way.

His mother shook her head. "You're forgetting, there are two beds in Kaylee's room, so there's no need for anyone to sleep on the couch."

"Yippeee! She can sleep in my room with me," Kaylee spoke up, stepping forward to place her hand in Sierra's. The child had no fear. Either that or she trusted in her Uncle Bruce's choice of friends.

Noah's expression darkened. "There's no way I'm letting someone I don't know sleep in my daughter's room."

"I wasn't suggesting she should. I'm suggesting *you* sleep in there, and Sierra can have your room. It's only temporary, Noah." His mother sent him a gaze that brooked no opposition, which only made Sierra feel worse for stopping by unannounced.

Noah let out a deep breath. "Fine. Your house, your rules." Noah's attitude was understandable, considering it was his daughter, and a stranger was in the house. At least, she was a stranger to him. Tank knew her, but his big brother had a lot at stake with Kaylee. His determination to not only protect but also teach the child moral values impressed Sierra.

It surprised her a little that Noah had gained some of her respect only by caring and loving his daughter. The whole respect-had-to-be-gained thing came from her father. The military had only compounded the belief that respect came from accomplishment—something twice as hard to get in the military. Sierra knew that much from personal experience.

"See. It's all good. Stay, Sierra. It'll be nice having you around," Tank said, leaning back against the porch railing.

Torn, Sierra tried to decide. She really did want to stay, even if Noah didn't want her here. Miles of farmland surrounding them gave her a sense of peace and quiet, and she was loath to give it up.

Even the house looked warm and welcoming. "I'll stay, but with one condition."

"What's that?" Tank asked, his brow raised in question.

"I want to help out with the chores on the ranch. Do my fair share. I'm not here to freeload, just to decompress."

"But your leg..." Noah was the first to speak up, but doubt was written on every face on the porch. Except Kaylee's. In her sweet innocence, she didn't understand.

Sierra held up her hand. "No buts. Do we have a deal?" This was Noah's chance to get rid of her, but she expected him to play nice if they all consented.

"I disagree. Company is not expected to work on the ranch," Laura said, the opposition coming from an unexpected source.

Sierra would never have made it to sergeant in the Army against all the men determined to prove they were better if she wasn't a little bit stubborn. Her father wasn't the only one with an attitude about women in the Army. "If we were talking about me staying just a day, I'd agree. But there's no reason I can't help if I'm going to be here for a bit. Of course, it depends on how long you all can suffer my presence."

"You were limping pretty bad earlier today, and you use a cane, not exactly ideal for ranch work. What if you hurt yourself further?" Sierra bristled at Noah's words.

Stay strong against adversity. Never weaken.

"I'm not an invalid, even though you insist on treating me like one. Sure, I may be slower than normal, but I can get the job done as well as the next person." Slow and painful was more like it, but the doc had said she needed to start trying to do more things and return to a more normal life. Ranch work could be a stretch, but ever since she'd turned eighteen, that's how she lived. *Determined to succeed.* More than anything, she didn't want the Jacksons to treat her differently. She wanted to earn their respect and prove she was capable of pulling her weight.

Maybe she felt this way because of Tank. After all—he'd witnessed her greatest failure. So perhaps this was a desire to prove herself worthy to him once again. And then there was Noah. He'd seen her weakness, and this was her way to prove to him she didn't need his pity. Why it mattered was unsettling and something she couldn't begin to fathom.

"Then let's get you moved in," Tank said, breaking the silence and the tension. "I'll get your bags and groceries. Kaylee, why don't you and your dad show Sierra to her room. Mom, if you fix a snack, we can all meet back up in fifteen minutes on the front porch to chat."

Sierra was grateful for her friend's attitude. She just didn't seem to have what it took these days to charge forward in any situation. Possibly because of Staff Sergeant Rhaegar. She missed her canine friend. As his handler, it was only right they be reunited here in the States, and she'd give anything to find him. Someone had to be able to trace what happened to him after he'd been flown home and discharged from the military due to his injuries.

The military wasn't exactly being cooperative, and it was infuriating. There were far too many handlers who'd tried and failed to find their K-9 partners, but she couldn't accept that possibility. Not yet. Not ever. Until she found him, Sierra could only hope he was safe and loved. She knew she had to remain hopeful, trusting in God to bring them together again.

"Miss Sierra, come and see my room." The little girl took her by the hand and led her down the hall. Luckily, the house was ranch style and therefore, a single story. The last thing she needed was Tank, or Noah, to have to carry her up the stairs.

They entered the bedroom, and Sierra was instantly sympathetic to Noah's plight. Twin beds. Ouch. No wonder the man wasn't happy about it. His well-over-six-foot-tall body would be crammed in like Goldilocks in Baby Bear's bed.

"What a pretty room," Sierra said, noting all the pretty pinks and lace. It was exactly the way her room had been at her mother's and father's insistence, and she'd hated every inch of it. On the other hand, Kaylee seemed to love it, beaming as she showed off her dolls, dress-up clothes, and tea-party dishes.

"Thank you. After we moved here, Daddy let me decorate it any way I wanted to. I've always wanted to be a princess."

"Sweetheart, you already are one. A princess is made in here," Sierra said, tapping her heart.

"You mean it? That's so cool! Daddy, Daddy, did you hear that? Miss Sierra says I'm a princess," Kaylee called out, her childlike exuberance heart-warming. It took so little to make a child happy.

It was the adults who were always the problem.

Chapter Three

♥

After dropping Kaylee off at Grover Elementary, Noah ran a few errands before returning to the house. His daughter found it difficult to go to sleep last night, her conversation and animation centered around the new house guest.

Kaylee was usually more reserved with strangers, and Noah considered the situation with mixed emotions. The last thing he needed was for Kaylee to get attached to Sierra. She wouldn't be in his daughter's life long, and the heartbreak Kaylee had been through when her mother left was more than enough for Noah to manage.

A quick check revealed no one was in the house. He had a feeling that Sierra was making good on her promise to help on the ranch. Bruce should have known better than to agree. But it appeared he hadn't been willing to argue with his sergeant, even if he wasn't serving in the military anymore. Once a soldier, always a soldier by the look of things.

Noah had no such hang-up. His concern was her injury. It didn't take someone with a doctorate to figure out she was in excruciating pain. And given she'd served with Bruce, it made sense she'd sustained the injury on the same mission Bruce had been on, the one that had changed his mind about staying in the military. At least, that's the way Noah saw it. His brother said he'd come home for a girl who lived in Boston, but Noah had yet to see or meet the mystery woman. With Sierra now in the picture, he was sure he knew why. His brother had already decided to move on. With Bruce, one never knew.

Determined to see firsthand how Sierra was faring, Noah headed to the barn. He spotted her mucking out one of the horse stalls. Kudos to her for agreeing to do it as it wasn't the most pleasant of jobs. What he didn't understand, was why his brother would let her—something he'd be sure to ask him later.

This was taking unfair advantage of a guest. Not only that, but it also didn't make sense Bruce would get her to muck out stalls if he was romantically interested. It wasn't exactly the way to a woman's heart, not even on a temporary basis, as was his brother's norm. Unless this was Bruce's way to even a score between them before they moved forward. Level the playing field, so to speak.

Noah watched her for a few moments, impressed with her strength. Not so much with her stride. She was limping, and without the use of her cane, it was more pronounced. The grimace on her face was a much better indicator. He didn't know her, but he could tell she was a proud woman, and hadn't liked his interfer- ence before. Nothing would have changed since then.

"Hey there," Noah said, coming up behind her and grabbing a pitchfork. "How's it going this morning?" With Sierra, he had a feeling the best way to help her was, well, to pitch in and help. *Literally.*

"Good morning. What are you doing?" Sierra asked, her eyes narrowing as he approached the next stall.

"Mucking stalls. It's my job. The question is, why are you doing my job? Not that I mind," he added for good measure, shooting her a grin.

"Tank said he normally does this. I was trying to lighten his load, not yours," she shot back. Honest to the core.

"We rotate." Noah shrugged. "Why don't we work on it together?" He lifted the first mound of manure-covered hay and chucked it in the wheelbarrow as if her answer didn't matter. Which it didn't. He wouldn't let her go it alone.

"Umm, I guess that's okay." She walked back to the stall she was working on, slower than before as if trying to hide her limp.

"While we work, we can talk. Why don't you tell me how you and my brother met? I can't help but be curious why you're here. My brother isn't known for women friends. Just girlfriends and ex-girlfriends." Bruce would kill him if he heard the comment. It wasn't like he was trying to warn her off his brother, was he?

Noah told himself it was just small talk, and if Sierra did the talking, and he worked extra fast, they'd be done in no time at all. Later, he'd talk with Bruce about what chores he got Sierra to take on in the future. This was far too strenuous, and not because she was a woman. She was injured, something his brother seemed foolishly unable to acknowledge.

She paused to look up at him, cocked her head to one side, and let out a deep breath as if coming to a decision. "We met four years ago when he enlisted. I was the K-9 handler assigned to his platoon. He's one of the few guys I've ever met that treats me as an equal. For that reason, we became friends. Good friends."

The way she said the last two words rankled Noah. He shouldn't care that his brother left a slew of women in his trail, but for some reason, he didn't want one of them to be Sierra. He'd only just met her, and so far, prickly and determined were the two best adjectives to describe her, but he liked the combination. Prickly was a self-defense mechanism he'd seen patients use time after time in the office. It didn't make her a bad person. In fact, the way she'd been with Kaylee last night was anything but bad. Kindhearted. That was another adjective he needed to add to the list.

"I see. My brother went through a rough patch before he was discharged. An attack in Afghanistan. Any chance you were serving with him then?"

"I was," she said, not bothering to elaborate.

"Is that where you were injured?"

"It is. I don't like to talk about it." Her voice grew more reserved. She stood up straight, leaning on the pitchfork and leveling him with her gaze. "So, if we're going to keep talking, we change the subject."

Noah kept working, pushing to finish the stall. "I can do that. Tell me about yourself. What do you like to do for fun?"

She shook her head and dug in for another scoop of manure. "Fun? I don't do fun. My whole adult life has been military. I signed up the day I turned eighteen and never looked back. Fun for me is military maneuvers or a hard run with a rucksack that tests my strength and tones my body. Or target practice. I'm always looking to improve my marksmanship. None of which I can do right now. Fun is overrated." Distress echoed in every sentence, exposing the depth of her feelings on the subject.

"Maybe it's time to set new fun parameters. What about hiking, skiing, kayaking, parasailing? There are any other number of things you can do to get out and enjoy nature. Explore something not from a military perspective, or with a gun," he added for good measure.

"Wouldn't know. And given my current condition, most of those are still out of the question. What about you? What do you do for fun?"

He hadn't meant to draw attention to her injury, but his efforts to make conversation had backfired. Only an idiot would suggest the things he had, especially not knowing the full extent of her injuries. "You've met Kaylee. Between work and her, there's not much time for my own fun, so I've learned to make do with her style of fun. I'm making memories with my daughter by going on picnics, playing games, and going horseback riding. And of course, playing with dolls and having tea parties. Things like that. Before I know it, she'll be grown, and these are times I can't get back." He didn't admit those last two activities very often, but it was different with Sierra for some reason. He didn't expect her to tease him about enjoying a tea party with his daughter.

"Wow. I'm impressed. I'm not sure I've even been on a picnic. If I did, I'm guessing it was forgettable." Sierra winced as she unloaded the last pitchfork of manure into the wheelbarrow.

Noah started toward her, but held back at the last second, turning for the wheelbarrow instead. "I'll haul the manure out of the barn and dump it. Maybe you should rest a minute or two while I finish this one."

She eyed him curiously, and he realized there were probably more stalls to be cleaned.

"There's more to do. I'll keep going while you dump that," Sierra said, her face scrunching up in distaste as she eyed the load of smelly manure.

Technically, Noah didn't work the ranch. He only helped on occasion. The physically demanding work wasn't new to him, but his job and Kaylee came first. "At least take a break, Sierra."

"I can't. I promised Tank I'd haul the fresh bales of hay into the stalls after this." She moved to the next one, emphasizing her point, and unwilling to rest for even a second.

Enough was enough. "Those bales weigh like fifty pounds. Don't you think that's overdoing it?"

Her eyebrows rose a notch. "I can lift a two-hundred-pound man and his gear and carry him off a field, I think I can manage a little ol' bale of hay."

Noah didn't budge from where he stood. "Maybe before you were injured, and maybe after you're healed."

"Why are you being such a He-Man and acting like I can't do things?" She huffed, not backing down.

Gumption. Sierra had a lot of it.

"I give up. I'm trying to get you to be smart about your injury, not irritate you."

His plan backfired as Sierra attacked the next stall with a ramped-up intensity to prove she could handle it. Why was it so hard for her to admit she wasn't operating at one hundred percent? It wasn't as if her injuries made her less of a person. Unless she felt like they did? That was entirely possible, but it was nothing he would ask her about, not after getting shut down repeatedly.

They worked in silence for the next fifteen minutes, Noah keeping a close eye on her. He noticed her holding the rail for support more often, but he knew he couldn't let her do this her way anymore when he saw her face. Her pained expression was more than he could bear, and whether she liked it or not, this madness had to end.

He rested his pitchfork against the stall wall and moved to her side. "Stop, Sierra. No more." Noah reached for her pitchfork, putting an end to the issue.

"I'm fine," she spouted, swinging around to glare at him. "Ouch," she cried out, reaching down to grab her leg and almost toppling over.

Noah caught her by the arm. "I've got you. Let me help."

"Just go away," she pleaded in a strained voice, pulling away from his grasp.

He was done playing by her rules. "Not a chance. Let's get you up to the house. You need to rest."

"Fine. But I can walk myself." Sierra put on a brave face and took a step, but the mask slipped as she crumpled to the ground.

Noah caught her around the waist and under her legs, swinging her up into his arms. "So can I. Anyone ever call you hardheaded?" He aimed for a light teasing tone, hoping to take her mind off the pain.

Her eyes misted, and he could tell she was fighting for self-control. She was fiercely determined to stand strong even while in pain. Sierra Winters was quite a woman.

"Thanks," she mumbled. "Maybe if you just let me rest and catch my breath, the throbbing will subside. It normally does." Sierra looked away, obviously not wanting him to see her face or let him read anything into her expression, but he'd already seen enough.

"Nope. You had your chance. Now we do this my way. And I've got a thing or two to say to Bruce about this. You have no business doing physical labor while you're recuperating from an injury." His brother needed help, but this was beyond reasonable, and he should've known better.

"Don't blame Tank. I asked what needed to be done and then told him which task I'd do. He didn't stand a chance against me." She shot him a half-grin, half-grimace.

"I totally understand that," Noah smirked, trying to keep their new camaraderie close at hand. It would make dealing with her a whole lot easier.

"You do?"

"Sure, I do. You're a convincing person." More like a woman any man would go out of his way to please.

"Thanks. That's a nice thing to say."

"Now that we're on the same page, will you tell me what's going on with the leg? What happened, and what's the diagnosis? What's your recuperation plan?" he asked as he walked toward the house, Sierra cradled in his arms.

"Are you a doctor or something?" she asked, gazing up at him, her arms locked around his neck.

"Or something," he teased, shooting her a wink.

"You know, if you want answers from me, you're going to need to be more forthcoming yourself. It's not a one-way-street, mister." Even now, her steely determination to get her way remained strong.

"I'm a nurse." There he'd said it. It might not come with all the glory of being a doctor, but for Noah, it was precisely what he wanted to be doing. The chance to make a difference in people's lives and be more personal. The opportunity to connect with patients.

Sierra shook her head, wearing more of a smile than grimace this time. "Nice try. So, Nurse Noah, the bomb that exploded left shrapnel in my calf bone. I've had a couple of failed surgeries, the last one four weeks ago. But it's taking its sweet time to heal. Hopefully, not much longer. My PT guy has me loaded up with physical therapy exercises, and I do them independently. Everyday."

"Seems to me it's going to take longer than expected because you won't stop long enough to let it heal." They made it back to the house, and Noah sat her down on the couch. "I'd like to take a look if you don't mind."

"I don't think that's nec—"

"It is necessary. Call it being overprotective, but I would do it for anyone. There's nothing wrong with caring about another human being, stranger or otherwise. Now, let me see it, Sierra." It was a great surprise when she gave in, pulling up her pant leg.

"Happy, Nurse Noah?" she asked with only a minimal amount of sarcasm.

He glanced at her calf and then back at her. "No. This is seriously inflamed. The surgical stitches closing the wound still look intact, but the area is red and swollen. I'm going to get you some ice and pain relievers, and then I expect you to elevate this and take it easy for the rest of the day. And I suggest you see a doctor about it."

Noah couldn't make her go, but he would make sure the family knew she had issues that prevented her from hard, physical labor, whether she wanted to pitch in or not. Correction. Whether she *demanded* to pitch in or not. Someone needed to override her decision, and it looked like that someone would be him.

Sierra folded her arms across her chest and let out a deep sigh. "You sure are bossy. But I'll think about it—the doctor thing, that is. And thank you, Noah. I'll do as you suggest and take it easy for a bit. I promise."

"Good girl." He stood up and retrieved a pillow to prop up her leg.

Her expression darkened. "So that's it? I'm a good girl because I'm giving in and I'm not strong enough to work through the pain?"

"No, good girl as in smart choice. Just like good boy. It's an expression." Her sudden change in attitude took him by surprise.

"Would you tell a military commander, good boy? You sound just like my father, and I've had enough mollycoddling all my life. Don't do that with me, and you and I will get along fine."

"Point taken. I stand corrected. Excellent choice, Sierra. I'll get you the ice, but then I've got to leave for work," he said, heading for the kitchen.

"Thank you. Out of curiosity, where is work for you?"

He paused at the doorway. Obviously, Sierra still didn't believe him and was trying to find out more. "At the hospital," Noah said, shooting her a grin as he left the room, leaving Sierra staring at him, her mouth hanging open in surprise.

Chapter Four

♥

SIERRA HADN'T COUNTED ON Noah showing up while she did her self-assigned chores. Her leg had been bothering her, and she knew she was overdoing it, but working alone, she didn't have to hide the pain. Just grimace, groan, and get the job done. One step at a time to prove herself.

It would have worked if Noah hadn't suddenly appeared looking as though he were a guardian angel sent to protect her from herself. She didn't believe his story about it being his turn to muck stalls, but Sierra was smart enough not to stop him from helping. Even though she hadn't given in gracefully, she appreciated his assistance.

The problem now, however, was that Noah knew too much of what was going on. He'd seen the nasty scar, red and swollen from overuse. She'd forgotten to tell him not to say anything to Tank, but she'd tell him tonight. She didn't want her squadmate to think she wasn't up to the task and start feeling sorry for her. Correction. *Ex-squadmate.*

She shifted the ice pack, the cold freezing against her skin—but at least it wasn't burning anymore. Laura was running an errand and had mentioned she'd be gone most of the day. Sierra had promised Noah no more chores, but they hadn't discussed easy cleaning around the house. She had to make herself useful. But with no one home and the deep ache in her leg, right now, a nap sounded far like a far better option.

"Miss Sierra, are you okay? I didn't know grown-ups took naps." Kaylee's question filtered through Sierra's brain. She opened her eyes, blinking a few times to discover the little girl peering down at her.

Sierra smiled, at least she did until it dawned on her it was after school hours if Kaylee was home. That meant she'd been asleep a lot longer than intended. She glanced at her watch. Three-thirty.

She'd had half a night's sleep, not a nap. Sitting up, only the slightest twinge of pain rippling down her leg. "Hi there. Sometimes grown-ups need naps, too. Did you have a good day at school?" she tried kickstarting her brain, but it was a sluggish process.

"I did. Rebecca Langley and me got to play at recess. She's my bestus friend. We formed a new club called the Little Princesses. I told her what you said, you know, about me being a princess and all. She wanted to be a princess too and so did some of the other girls, so we formed the club." Kaylee's eyes were lit with excitement as she relayed her day. Fitting in was important, and it was terrific she had sweet friends. They all seemed to be filled with the same youthful exuberance.

"Kaylee, I asked you not to bother Sierra," Laura said from the kitchen doorway.

"I'm not bothering her. I promise. I just asked her why she was sleeping. And she asked me about my day." Kaylee's face was the picture of innocence.

"It's okay, Laura. I can't believe I slept that long. I don't sleep well at night, so it took me by surprise."

Other than in the hospital, Sierra couldn't remember taking an afternoon nap since she was five.

"Maybe what you need is more naps then. At least, until you get the night hours figured out. When it comes to healing, it does a body good to get some sleep." Laura crossed the room to her side. "Is there anything I can get you? The ice pack had fallen on the floor, so I put it away. Would you like it again?" She fluffed the pillows, offering one to Sierra.

"Thanks," Sierra said, pushing the pillow behind her back into a comfortable position. "And, no, I don't need a thing. But thank you. My leg acts up sometimes. It'll be okay." She had been praying for a long time, that one day, there wouldn't be so much pain. And preferably no limp. The biggest problem at this point was she was getting in her own way of the healing process—like today. And Noah had seen right through her.

"Okay, then. If you're sure. I'm going to get started on some dinner, and I'll take Kaylee into the kitchen with me so she can't bother you. You just relax and make yourself right at home, dearie." Laura held out her hand for Kaylee, reinforcing her words.

Kaylee pulled back. "But I want to stay with Miss Sierra," she said, her little girl voice tinged with a slight whine.

Sierra didn't want to cause problems. "How about I come to the kitchen? Maybe I can make myself useful and clean up as you cook, and Kaylee can do homework if she has any." Sierra stood, sucking in a deep breath as the familiar ache intensified and sliced down her leg.

"I don't have homework, silly. I'm only seven. We get fun play sheets," Kaylee said, shaking her head.

Sierra admired the teacher's creativity in coming up with a new twist for what was simply homework. "That's cool. Then maybe you can color, and we can all have a little kitchen party." She shot Laura a wink, hoping she'd go along with the plan.

"A kitchen party? That sounds fun. I'll be right back." Kaylee raced out of the room and down the hall toward her bedroom.

Laura grinned. "Sounds to me like Kaylee's got you wrapped around her little finger, and you've only been here a day."

Sierra followed her into the kitchen. "Not wrapped—not yet anyway." She laughed. "It's hard to resist her sweetness, and it's nice to feel wanted."

Laura tied on an apron. "Wrapped. Call it what it is. She does that with all of us. However, I am surprised she took to you so quickly," she said, opening up the cookbook and flipping through the pages.

Sierra wasn't sure how to take the comment. "Why? Do I come across as an ogre?"

Laura looked up and smiled. "No, and I'm sorry. That came out wrong. Kaylee takes a while to warm up to strangers. Ever since her mother left, she's been quite introverted with new people. I've been a bit worried, but my worry is almost gone after seeing her around you. She's a loving child, and I wouldn't want her to lose that because her mother hurt her by getting a divorce and moving on with her own life. Kaylee's a good judge of character, the way I see it."

The compliment caught Sierra unaware, and her cheeks flushed warm. "Poor thing. Doesn't her mother see her at all?" It was easier to avoid the part about Kaylee's seeming attachment to her, instead of focusing on what mattered. Sierra knew what it felt like to be unwanted, but she still had both parents in the picture. Her father, for all his gruffness and lofty expectations, wasn't a bad guy deep down. He just wasn't someone she agreed with—about anything.

Laura began to pull different ingredients out and lay them on the counter. "She left them almost a year ago and has only come to see Kaylee twice. Calls about once a month. Noah tells me it's some highfalutin job of hers that keeps her busy. Sounds like an excuse if you ask me. I think it's awful, but don't pay any attention to me and my opinions. I'm biased."

"Hardly a biased opinion. Not many would disagree. It sounds like Kaylee's mother's not someone worthy of the overflowing love and zest Kaylee has for life. I'm guessing she'll outgrow this stage of emotional turmoil." At least Sierra hoped she would. She made a mental note to add Kaylee to her prayer list.

"It looks to me like she already is, thanks to you."

There it was again. Respect. Honor. Admiration. All things she wanted but had done nothing to deserve. "Time will tell." Agreeing with Laura didn't seem right...but then, neither did disagreeing.

"Why don't you help me cook? If you're sure the leg is doing okay, that is? It's more fun to cook together with someone, and the boys aren't much help."

Sierra winced. "*Ummm*, I should stick with the cleaning. Trust me on this one."

Laura looked over at her in surprise. "Why is that? Don't you like to cook?"

Sierra felt warmth flood her cheeks. She was a trained soldier and a canine handler, but when it came to the kitchen, she was useless. The last thing she wanted to do was admit to such a weakness, but she didn't see that she had much choice. "It's not so much that I don't like to cook, I just don't know how to." She waited to see the loss of respect in the woman's eyes.

Laura shrugged. "Tonight's dinner isn't fancy or anything. Easy-peasy, macaroni and tomatoes on toast. And for dessert, warm chocolate melting cake and vanilla-bean ice cream." There was surprise in Laura's eyes, but that was it. No sudden distancing as if Sierra had suddenly become useless and excess baggage.

"Sounds complicated. And messy. You'll need someone to do the dishes, and I'm just the right person for that duty." There was no way she wanted Laura to know the whole truth. She never cooked. Ever.

"The dishes will get done; don't you worry. But first, here's the recipe. I'll get out the ingredients, and you can start to brown the hamburger meat." Laura pointed to a laminated card on the counter and handed Sierra the meat from the refrigerator. She wasn't taking no for an answer.

With no choice in the matter, unless she wanted to be rude, Sierra turned the burner on high and dumped the square lump in the pan. She spotted a spatula in a canister nearby and grabbed it, hoping to make it look like she knew what she was doing.

Laura found the few last ingredients needed and lined them up on the counter in the order they appeared on the card. The woman must have the recipe memorized, which was quite impressive.

Kaylee burst into the kitchen. "What's for dinner?"

"Macaroni and tomatoes on toast. And Sierra's cooking for us. Isn't that a nice treat?" Laura smiled at her granddaughter. "You can sit right up here and do your sheets, maybe even learn a few cooking tips from Sierra." Laura pulled back a bar stool, and Kaylee hopped up onto the seat.

"I can't wait for supper," Kaylee said. Laura was good with the little girl. Always interactive and the special bond between them showed.

But as for Kaylee learning by watching Sierra, the woman couldn't be more wrong. The poor girl and her grandmother might have to eat their words for dinner because tonight's meal might not be edible with Sierra at the helm. She wasn't even sure how she'd been roped into cooking and not just helping. Something about not being an ungracious guest, but this didn't bode well—for anyone.

"I'll be right back. I'm going to get you an apron, dearie." Laura headed through the door, and Sierra turned back to the task at hand, hoping she was getting this part right.

The oil in the pan spit out, biting her arm, and popping at her repeatedly. Smoke started rising from the frying pan. Thinking it was time to flip the block of meat, she grabbed the spatula and turned it over. Oil spattered upward, and Sierra jumped back to avoid getting burnt. The grease landed on the burner, causing more smoke to fill the kitchen.

"Turn off the burner. It's too hot," Kaylee said, sliding off her chair and backing away. *Smart move, kiddo.*

"What in heaven's name..." Laura said, rushing back into the room. She grabbed hold of the pan and slid it to the side, turning the burner down.

"I'm sorry. It started popping right out of the pan. I've made a mess. Here, you take over, and I'll clean it up," Sierra said, on the verge of tears. Even a seven-year-old had a better grasp of what to do. But then the seven-year-old embraced her feminine side in a way Sierra had never done. Being tough and strong and the best she could be didn't include girly stuff like cooking. At least, that's what Sierra had believed her entire life.

"Nonsense." Laura ignored her request and didn't take the spatula. "I've turned it down. Medium heat is a good browning temperature. Use your spatula and break the meat up into little crumbled pieces." She pushed Sierra's hand back toward the pan encouragingly.

Doing as instructed, she broke apart the meat, pleased the oil wasn't popping out at her. *Mental note: heat too high with oil hurts*. So much for being the brave soldier. Her father would have laughed her right out of the kitchen and then gone to great pains to remind her for years to come of her failure.

"Like this?" she asked. The meat was half brown and spread out, and Sierra stirred it around, common sense telling her she needed to or else only the bottom half of the beef would brown.

Laura came back to her side to check the progress. "Absolutely. So, when you said you don't like to cook, did you really mean you don't cook?"

Put on the spot, she wouldn't lie or sidestep the issue. It's not like Laura couldn't see the truth. "That's exactly what I meant, as in, not at all. I'm sorry. I should have told you before you left the room." Sierra felt like an idiot.

"It's not a big deal, but perhaps something that needs rectifying," Laura said without a trace of disappointment lacing her voice.

"What's rec-recifying?" Kaylee asked, cocking her head to one side, her forehead scrunched tightly as she considered the big word.

"Rectifying is fixing a situation," Laura explained.

"Fixing's good. Just like Miss Sierra's leg needs rec-rectifying." Kaylee beamed, pleased with her use of the word.

"Not quite the same, but close enough." Sierra grinned, suddenly not feeling quite as awful about what she'd done. It was a failure that didn't seem to bother anyone.

"So how is it you don't cook? You eat, don't you?" Laura laughed.

"I do eat. But growing up, my mother had the honor of cooking and didn't like me in the kitchen. Probably because when I did help, I made a mess and ruined everything. In the military, the mess hall took the place of my mother. And since I was injured, it's been hospital food and back to my mother's. Full circle." The only thing she didn't mention was that she'd ruined things on purpose growing up. Not the case today—that had been a pure lack of talent.

Laura's brow tightened. "Sounds to me like your mother wasn't as patient as she could've been. Young children make messes. It goes with the territory. I remember it wasn't easy when I taught the boys. They still prefer me to cook, but they aren't afraid to pitch in when they need to."

"Grandma laughs at me when I get flour everywhere. She says it's half the fun," Kaylee chimed in.

Perhaps it was time for a little truth. It wasn't all Sierra's mother's fault, and she couldn't let her take the blame. "It was a little more than that. You see, I didn't want to cook. I wanted to be outside playing with the boys. Fishing, skipping rocks, riding dirt bikes. Anything other than being in the kitchen. Let's just say it wasn't my thing. I went above and beyond to make sure my mother exiled me from the kitchen." It felt good to speak the truth.

"*Tsk-tsk*. Everyone needs to know how to cook. Male and female. It's a necessary life skill. Besides, you won't always be in the military." It was odd. Laura was calling her out, but for some reason, Sierra didn't mind.

It was something she'd have to think about later, but right now, she had a meal to prepare. "True. I've just never needed the skill."

"Sounds like a good time to start with the basics." Laura was right. Everyone needed to eat and should be able to manage simply dishes. She could do this. Would do this. And she suspected Laura wasn't going to let her off the hook anyway. Besides, Sierra always loved a challenge, and that's how she would look at cooking. "Okay, then teach away."

"Can I show Miss Sierra some of my special toys while she cooks?" Kaylee asked.

"Sounds like a great plan." Laura nodded and moved to the pantry as Kaylee skipped out of the kitchen.

"What's first?" Sierra was going all-in on this challenge.

"You've already learned about meat and oil," Laura said, grinning as she laid several tomatoes on the counter. "I've laid everything out. Now, go down the list one by one and add the spices to the meat. Once that starts to simmer, you can add the tomatoes last, and then you're done with the main course until it's time to cook the pasta and mix it all together. This is one of those heat-and-eat-when- ready meals, meaning it's time to eat whenever the guys show up."

Laura made it sound so easy, which worked for Sierra. The pain in her leg kept increasing, and it was getting more difficult to hide her anguish. The last thing she wanted to do was ruin her first kitchen party. "Really? That's all there is to it? There's not much going in here."

"It doesn't take much if the ingredients are right—just like a relationship. Throw in something wrong, and it's a disaster." Talk about going off track.

Sierra assumed she was talking about Kaylee's mother and it would seem there was no love lost between the two women. "I wouldn't know. I've been too focused on the military to worry about relationships, so it's safe to say I'm not in the marital market." It was a warning just in case Laura had gotten the wrong idea.

"Well, maybe it's time for more of both in your life."

And there it was—the reason for the warning. Sierra had a strange feeling Laura was talking about Kaylee and Noah. "Both?" Sierra couldn't help but ask.

"Cooking and relationships." Laura winked. "You finish that, and I'll get the dessert ingredients out. It's another easy recipe you're going to love making, and love eating even more. That is if you like chocolate." She breezed right past the relationship comment and moved back to cooking with untold finesse.

"Oh, I like chocolate." This was turning out to be fun. Laura knew exactly what to say to encourage her, and Sierra flourished under her tutelage.

Kaylee came back, her arms loaded with stuffed animals and dolls. "This one is my bestest ever. He's a monkey like Curious George, except better, cause he's mine. His name is Mr. Snuggles. My daddy got him for me when I got curious bout something and went exploring. I fell and cut my leg wide open." Kaylee used her hands to point at a six-inch line, which by the look of it, would have been painful. It was something they had in common.

"But it's okay now, right?" Sierra asked in concern.

"Yup. Daddy and Mr. Snuggles healed me all up. I was in the hospital and everything," she said, her eyes growing wide. The hospital wasn't Sierra's favorite place, but it was a badge of honor to Kaylee. Sierra felt like it was a badge of defeat.

One by one, Sierra heard a detailed story about every stuffed animal. By the time Kaylee finished, dinner was ready. Sierra had cooked her first meal and prepped dessert. Almost.

"Dinner smells great." Laura beamed, peering at the frying pan and the simmering casserole.

"The chocolate batter is de-lic-ous." Kaylee took another swipe from the bowl they'd given her as a treat.

"Don't tell the guys I made dinner," Sierra asked. "I want to see what they say without them pouring on heavy compliments because they feel they have to."

"Fair enough." Laura nodded. "But they are going to love it, so no worries."

"I like a good secret," Kaylee exclaimed, her face wreathed in a smile.

"Good deal," Sierra agreed, a little nervous but looking forward to the guys' honest reactions.

"I'm going to set the table. If you want to toss everything in the sink, we'll be done until after dinner. That's when the beauty of cooking really shines best." Laura grinned, removing her apron.

"What do you mean?"

"Because whoever cooked doesn't have to clean."

Laura laughed and headed for the dining room with a stack of plates in hand.

"Miss Sierra, can I ask you something?" Kaylee asked.

"Of course, honey. What is it?"

"I'm going to enter the goat-chasing contest at the Veteran's Day Jubilee. I'm the fastest runner in my class, and I'm going to win. I simply *have to* beat Tommy Thompkins. He's a boy who lives in town who thinks he's the fastest, and he keeps telling me girls aren't as fast as boys." Kaylee's face scrunched up in disgust.

"He's wrong. Girls can be just as fast. It doesn't mean they all are, but they can be. There's a difference." Something she'd learned the hard way and through a determination to succeed.

"I don't know what that means, but will you come and watch me race?" Kaylee turned imploring eyes upon her and waited, her hopeful expression not one Sierra could resist.

Laura was right, Kaylee did have her wrapped. The problem was, Veteran's Day was two weeks away. "I don't know, honey. I might not be here then." The truth was, Sierra wasn't sure what she'd be doing. If she wasn't any good helping out at the ranch, she didn't feel it was right to impose on the Jackson family.

"Please?" Kaylee whined. "You're in the Army like my Uncle Bruce used to be. He's big and strong, so you must be big and strong too. We can show Tommy how wrong he is, and you can cheer me on when I beat him."

Kaylee had managed to zero in on Sierra's Achille's heel. Boys versus girls in the age-old battle of the sexes. "Sure thing, honey. I'll be there."

"Pinky promise?" Kaylee asked.

"Pinky promise." Even if she moved on from here, she'd make a point of coming back to the jubilee for Kaylee.

"Yay, and then you can go to the ball with me after and see me in my fairy princess dress. I bet you have a really pretty dress too," Kaylee exclaimed, her eyes wide and twinkling with delight.

A ball? That was way more than Sierra had bargained for, but she didn't have it in her heart to take it back and say no.

Chapter Five

♥

IT WAS A TWENTY-FIVE-MINUTE drive home from the hospital, and Noah was looking forward to seeing Kaylee. She was always a bundle of energy, and he enjoyed her antics, even if they were all-consuming. Days like today were his favorite. A short day at work made it easier to spend time with her, and it made up for the fact that tomorrow was his late- night, and she'd most likely be in bed when he got home.

He pulled into the driveway, and within seconds, Kaylee ran out of the house to greet him. Noah scooped her up into his arms. "How's my little girl today?"

"I had a good day at school, Daddy. I made a new friend, and we made a princess club and everything. And then when I got home, I had even more fun with Grandma and Miss Sierra." That explained the extra glow on his daughter's face.

"That's great. You'll have to tell me more about your special club over dinner. Is it ready yet?"

"I think so. And we have a *very* special dinner for you and Uncle Bruce." Kaylee's emphasis on the word "very" drew his attention. It was like one of her secretive girly comments used when she and his mother were up to something.

"Because of Miss Sierra?" he asked, figuring it was worth a shot.

"I pinky promised not to say a word," she said, using her fingers to zip her lips.

Noah smiled. Exactly as he'd expected. He'd have to be careful where Kaylee and Sierra were concerned. It wouldn't do to have his daughter get all buddy-buddy with her when Sierra could blow out of their lives as fast as she'd blown in. Although, judging by his daughter's enthusiasm at the moment, it might already be too late. Kaylee wouldn't understand when Sierra left. The same way she still didn't understand why her own mother didn't take time to see or talk to her.

The other issue, of course, was that Noah was having the same problem as his daughter. All day he'd found himself thinking about Sierra. Her injury was significant. It would be a complicated wound to heal since she seemed determined not to rest it. He was worried about her. At least, that was the only reasonable explanation to his interest.

Sierra stepped out on the porch. "Do you mind if I have a word with you?" It was as if thinking about her made her appear. Another reason to quit thinking about her, he inwardly chuckled.

She came down the steps, slow and cautious, not bothering to wait for his answer. It's not like he'd say no, and she knew it. "Sure thing. Kaylee, honey, can you let your grandmother know I'm home."

"Okay, Daddy. But, Miss Sierra, don't be long. You know, we have that *thing* in the kitchen to do." Kaylee grinned.

Sierra held a finger to her lips. "I remember. I'll be right in." Noah had no idea what they were talking about but judging by how much fun they seemed to be having with the secrecy, asking questions wouldn't get him any answers.

Kaylee went inside, the screen door slamming closed behind her.

"What's up? And how's the leg?" Noah asked the question to try and stay focused on the reason for his interest—as if to prove it to himself.

"That's what I want to talk to you about. I took your advice and rested it, and it's doing better. Thank you."

She hadn't rested it enough, judging by the limp when she came across the porch and down the steps.

"That's good." He nodded, waiting for her to continue. Sierra was a tough woman, but why she felt the need to hide her pain was beyond him. People didn't have to be tough all the time, and her injuries earned her the right to some sympathy.

"Listen, *ummm...* I'd really like it if you didn't say anything to your brother about earlier today. It's hard to explain, but I outranked him when we served together, and we're friends. I don't want things to be awkward between us if he starts worrying. I don't want to lose his respect. That is, if I haven't already." She mumbled the last bit, but Noah heard her.

He'd dealt with enough patients to know what was going on. Sierra felt responsible for what happened on the mission that had disastrous results, but what he didn't understand, was why.

Hopefully, she would talk to someone about what had happened in Afghanistan. He fixed bodies, not minds. His brother was proof of that. Noah hadn't been able to help Bruce when he'd come home, but things were different now. And Noah couldn't help but think Sierra was the cause. for his brother's positive change in attitude.

"Your secret is safe with me, although I can't agree with why you find it necessary. Bruce will only want to help you, and an injury doesn't diminish one's power or strength inside. It's what's in your heart that matters most." *Shut up, Noah. You sound like you're giving her relationship advice instead of emotional support.*

His brother and Sierra must be special friends. The thought that they might be friends with benefits caused a twinge of unwarranted jealousy to rifle through him. Noah and Sierra had shared a moment this morning, but it had been a friendly moment. That's all that ever could be between them for a multitude of reasons, especially considering the old rule of never dating a brother's love interest—past or current.

"That's where you're wrong. What matters is what you can and can't do. My father taught me that at an early age. Respect is earned by achievements and being the best, and you can't earn it if you can't do things." Sierra's way of thinking, albeit from her father, explained a lot about her. And from where he stood, it wasn't a good line of reasoning.

"Your father has an interesting way of thinking." Noah frowned.

"Tell me about it," Sierra said, rolling her eyes.

"But I disagree with him. Respect is earned. And it can be earned by doing things, but not in the sense that respect is a payment for services given or simply by scaling the highest mountain. It's the heart recognizing whatever's been done as special, including mutual acknowledgment of one another's feelings, wishes, and traditions. It's called caring." It was something his mother had taught him, and it had served him well over the years and in his line of work.

Sierra tensed, crossing her arms in front of her chest. "We'll have to agree to disagree. It's a little more straightforward than a heart's recognition, which is something one can't see."

Kaylee pushed open the screen door. "Grandma says you two need to come inside and wash up. Dinner will be ready in a few minutes."

"Where's Uncle Bruce?" Noah asked, taking a step toward the porch. He'd like to hear more on Sierra's viewpoint some other time, and even try to convince her she was wrong.

"He's in the shower. Singing. He's not very good," Kaylee said, scrunching up her face.

"Kaylee..."

"I know. I know. If I don't have anything nice to say, I shouldn't say anything at all," his daughter mumbled and turned to go back into the house.

"Thank you. Tell Grandma we're coming right this minute." It didn't matter how good or bad his brother's voice was—the singing itself showed signs of improvement in Bruce's attitude. More proof Sierra's presence was affecting his brother in a good way.

He turned and offered Sierra a hand to help her up the steps. Her steely and non-appreciative gaze bore into him until he dropped his hand. Point taken. The prickly woman didn't like help, but her tough-as-nails exterior was only a façade, and he'd seen a part of the real person she was this morning. Did Bruce? Or did his brother only see what Sierra let the rest of the world see?

It was more like ten minutes later by the time they were all seated around the table. Kaylee and Sierra had mysteriously disappeared into the kitchen, where he'd been told he couldn't go.

More of the girl-bonding time he was worried about. Later, he'd talk with Sierra and set the record straight to make sure she understood his concerns. For now, dinner was served and seeing as it was macaroni and tomatoes on toast, everything else could wait.

Noah took a few bites, and then a few more. Tonight, the casserole was even more delicious than he remembered. Either that, or he was even more hungry than he'd realized. "This is great, Mom. One of your best," he said, scooping up another forkful.

Kaylee giggled and slapped a hand over her mouth.

Bruce shrugged. "I agree, but right now, I don't care what's in front of me as long as it's food."

"Well, thanks a lot," his mom said, giving Bruce the stink eye. "I think for that comment alone, you should lose your dessert. I'm sure the rest of us wouldn't mind polishing off your share of warm chocolate melting cake," she admonished, a smile on her face.

Noah glanced over at Bruce and smirked. "Tough luck, bro. More for me."

"What? I didn't say anything bad. I mean, it's good. It's food. How is that a terrible thing?" Bruce scowled, digging in for another bite. "Women," he added, frustrated by the turn of events.

"Because Miss Sierra made it," Kayla exclaimed, bouncing in her seat, eager to share the secret. A secret that explained all the earlier comments, giggles, and special looks.

Bruce had really stepped into a manure pile on this one. Serves him right. "I noticed it was different," Noah said. "Great job, Sierra." They say the way to a man's heart is through his stomach, and Noah wished for the second or third time since Sierra had shown up that he had a heart to give, or at the very least, one he trusted to make the right decisions.

"Thank you," she murmured, her cheeks flushing prettily.

"Personal recipe?" Noah asked, taking an interest in her efforts to help with dinner. It was nice of her.

Sierra and his mother burst out laughing. He looked at his brother and shook his head, not knowing what was going on between them. What he couldn't fail to notice, however, was that his mother and Sierra seemed different. Closer. Co-conspiratorial.

His mother. The woman who had not liked Blanche from the day she'd met her, although she'd tried her best not to let it show. She'd always believed in letting her sons make their own decisions and living with the consequences. And divorce was an enormous consequence.

"No, nothing like that. It was more a case of some of this and some of that, using your mom's recipe." Sierra looked down at her plate and used her fork to toy with her food.

"I don't follow?" This was above his pay grade. Women and their little secrets.

"I didn't know you could cook, Sierra," Bruce said baldly.

She looked up at his brother and shrugged. "I can't, but your mom wanted to give me a cooking lesson, and I accepted. Sort of." Sierra laughed. "It's not like I had a choice."

"She did, huh?" Noah looked at his brother, his frown deepening.

"Mom?" Bruce questioned, looking back and forth between the two women. Clearly, he was just as shocked as Noah.

"Everyone should know how to cook a few good meals. Poor Sierra never had the opportunity while growing up or in the military, and I aim to correct the oversight." His mother explained it as though it were a completely normal thing for her to do, something he and his brother knew wasn't true.

"You do?" Noah uttered, still surprised. Blanche had turned out to be his mother's least favorite of her sons' girlfriends, but looking back, none of them had really hit it off with his mother. Sierra was a first.

"I do." His mother nodded.

"And I've accepted, at least while I'm visiting." Sierra smiled. It was a beautiful smile born of sweet truth and honest emotion.

"She's staying till the Veterans' Day Jubilee. Remember, Miss Sierra." Kaylee looked to her for confirmation.

"I remember, but I'm not sure I can stay that long. Things have changed a bit...with my injury...and it would seem ranch work is harder than I'd expected in my condition. I'm not good at sitting around, and I wouldn't want to overstay my welcome. I can always come back for the jubilee, though." It was a significant first step in Sierra's recovery—admitting she wasn't up to speed.

"She promised, Daddy. A pinky promise," Kaylee added.

"That's a big promise." Noah grinned, knowing to Kaylee it was the ultimate promise. "But I don't understand just what she agreed to do."

"Miss Sierra is coming to the Veteran's Day Jubilee to watch me win the goat-chasing race. I told you about the race. Remember, Daddy? And she's coming to the ball with me. She's the best." She looked expectantly at her new best friend for confirmation.

Sierra nodded.

Of course, Noah knew about the celebration, but Sierra's involvement was an update he didn't welcome. The event was still two weeks away and there wasn't a chance his daughter wouldn't have fallen in love with Sierra by then. Heck, *he'd* have a tough time not falling for her. The only difference was, he knew what to do with his feelings and how to manage them. The ignore button worked well. But Kaylee was a child, and she wouldn't understand why getting attached to Sierra was not a promising idea.

"I do. But I also remember telling you it's not about winning. It's about having fun. Everyone who enters will win and get an award." Noah had to rein in his daughter before she went too far with the whole winning thing, *or* with the whole Sierra thing.

"I know. I know." She huffed out a deep breath. "But I'll still know I came in first—and so will Tommy. Right, Miss Sierra?"

"Kaylee—" Noah tried to stop this line of thought.

"Right, Kaylee. Winning is great but do make sure you have fun either way. There's no guarantee you'll win, but it'll make you try harder next time if you don't. Practice more, get better," Sierra said, once again confirming her belief that winning was ultimately everything.

"She's seven, Sierra." Noah had heard enough. "I don't want her to lose sight of what's important— having fun. And she's my daughter..." He left the rest unsaid, hoping she would receive the message loud and clear. *Butt out.*

Sierra stiffened at the rebuke.

"Well, if anyone knows about winning, it's Sierra. She always pushed herself to be better than every guy in the platoon," Bruce spoke up, but his words offered little comfort to Noah and his efforts to teach his daughter a valuable lesson.

"That's not true," Sierra countered with a shake of her head.

"Is too. I remember once when you lost out in a run by mere seconds, and for the next two weeks, you trained harder than ever," Bruce said, rebuking her efforts to discount the truth. "Until you beat him out."

Hence the athletic figure and win-at-all-costs attitude. There wasn't an ounce of powder puff inside Sergeant Sierra Winters. And that was the key to her prickly attitude.

"If I can change the subject… Sierra, you can stay as long as you like. It's nice having another woman around to talk with. All this male testosterone can be a bit much, and I for one, think it will be grand to have you attend the jubilee and the ball with our family," his mother said.

Noah couldn't believe what he was hearing. He and Kaylee weren't the only ones in the Sierra Winters' fan club. In fact, by the looks of things, the entire family was in the same club.

"Thank you, Laura, but I'm going to see what happens. I report back for duty December 6th, and I need to go home at some point." Not that she was looking forward to spending much time at home leading up to the Thanksgiving holiday.

Bruce leaned back in his chair and pushed his plate back. "Have you heard anything about Rhaegar?"

"Who's Rhaegar?" Kaylee interjected before stuffing another bite of the casserole in her mouth.

Noah instantly recognized the change in Sierra when Bruce asked the question. He waited for the answer, sure it would be another clue to unraveling the Sierra mystery he found himself caught up in.

She drew in a deep breath. "Rhaegar is a black German shepherd who was in the military, and I was his handler. He's also my best friend. Staff Sergeant Rhaegar was discharged from the Army a month ago, after he was injured in the line of duty. The people who oversaw the transport back to the U.S. lost track of him. I'm told he was healthy and sent somewhere to wait out my recovery so I could adopt him, but somehow, they lost track of where he was sent. I've spent the last three weeks trying to find him, but to no avail. I miss him terribly." Sierra choked on the last words.

"With your determination, I'm sure you'll find him," Noah said, accepting the subject's peaceful change. Sierra's comment added another piece to the puzzle, and his heart ached for all she'd been through. His brother still had PTSD episodes, and he wondered how Sierra was dealing with every-thing.

Not only as a woman in the military, but also because of Rhaegar.

"You must be so sad to have your doggy lost." Kaylee got down from her seat and went around the table to give Sierra a hug.

"I'll find him, hon. Don't worry." Sierra gave his daughter a brave smile, but he could tell her heart was breaking.

A look passed between his brother and Sierra, one reserved for two people connected on a different level. Was it their shared past? Or a shared future?

Chapter Six

♥

SIERRA'S INTERNAL CLOCK WENT off much the same way it had for the past ten years. Military training and military time meant waking at dawn. She rubbed her leg, the throbbing ache ramping up the minute her feet hit the ground. Sitting on the bed, she reached for her pain pills and the glass of water on the nightstand. Knocking two tablets back, she hoped they would kick in sooner rather than later.

She glanced around Noah's room. He'd moved back here six months ago from what she understood, but it was only temporary. That explained why the place was void of personal effects, unlike Kaylee's room. The little girl must have brought everything she owned with her, while Noah appeared to limit himself to clothes. The only personal touch in the room was a photo of Kaylee.

The room was sterile in appearance and could have doubled as a hotel room—with the exception of the two paintings on the wall, that is. The vibrant splashes of color in the landscape renderings captured her eye, making it feel as though she were walking right into the wooded forest. Her best guess would be that his mother would have been the one to add the special touches. Sierra didn't think Noah would be the kind of guy with an eye for decorating. She smiled, grateful the pain meds were kicking in.

Somewhere in the middle of the night, she'd made the decision to take more of Noah's advice and see if she could score an appointment at the Veteran's hospital this morning. She was supposed to have regular check-ins so the reports could be sent back to her commanding officer. Something she hadn't done because driving back to Boston wasn't a high priority.

Noah was right, of course. She'd overdone it yesterday. The past couple of days, truthfully. It wasn't that she was stubborn though—he was wrong about that. She liked to think of it as a determination to heal and return to normal, or as normal as she could, given the metal plate in her leg used to strengthen the bone.

The PTSD flashbacks came less often now, and what she really needed was peaceful walks in the woods, a place to reflect. Like the one in the painting. A place to get lost and forget the world all around her.

Sierra heard a noise in the house and got up to investigate. Another early-bird riser meant someone to have coffee with. As she padded down the hall- way, using her cane for support, she caught the sound of the front door closing just as she entered the living room. So much for a coffee partner. She moved to the front window, trying to see who was up this early. More than likely, Tank was still on the same schedule as she was.

Her friend seemed to be doing well, although, at odd moments, she caught him staring off into space. Much the same way she did if she was remembering the blast that had claimed the lives of one of their comrades. Tank busied himself on the ranch all day, leaving little time for them to talk. On purpose, perhaps?

She shouldn't have come here.

It wasn't a good move for either one of them. But Sierra missed Tank's friendly face and odd sense of humor and needed his support. She'd turned to him because he understood her and expected nothing more than she was willing to give. It started and ended with friendship.

Not that Tank hadn't tried to put the moves on her occasionally when they were off duty. It was inappropriate given her rank, but it was more than that. Sierra wasn't interested in a relationship because most men couldn't handle a tough female. It was like it brought up every ounce of competitive spirit they possessed, their desire to prove themselves worthy almost ridiculous.

She also simply wasn't attracted to Tank that way. *Not like I am to Noah.* Sure, Noah was handsome, but it was more than that. It was his kind spirit, his big heart, his caring... The list went on. And not once had he shown a fierce need to prove himself as stronger or better. Just more caring and perceptive. She'd seen right through his ploy to help her in the stalls and appreciated it even more since he hadn't said a word, making up some song and dance story in an effort not to upset her.

But no matter how long the list of his positive attributes got, it wouldn't change anything. Sierra still wasn't looking for a relationship. Her job as a dog handler in the military gave her all the connection she needed. And it was the reason she'd never be promoted over her current rank. She didn't want to lead men, just work with the dogs. Not to mention, after the mistake in Afghanistan, it was clear she shouldn't be trusted with the soldier's lives.

You and Rhaegar saved most of the squad.

The voice of reason echoed in her head, vying to be heard. "But it wasn't enough," she mumbled out loud. *One loss was one too many.*

She poured a cup of coffee and made her way back down the hall. A quick shower and a phone call later, she felt better knowing she had an appointment with Dr. Alfonzo later that morning.

Sierra waited for Kaylee to leave for school before heading to the VA hospital in Lancaster. It gave her time to think about the future, something she'd been putting off since returning home. The military was the only life she'd known. Except now, life as she knew it, was in jeopardy.

Short of a miracle, there was a good chance of reassignment and she wouldn't be training with the dogs anymore. Which wouldn't have been so bad it if weren't for the fact she wasn't cut out for a desk job, and because she still hadn't found Rhaegar. Not having another dog to fill the void in her heart would tear her to pieces. Not that Rhaegar was replaceable. Only that another dog would force her to open her heart again to form a new team, the two living and working together 24/7.

Her contract was almost up for renewal, which left leaving the military altogether as another option—her least favorable one. And when and if she did leave, there was one solid truth Laura had pointed out, she needed to learn how to cook. So, for as long as Sierra stayed here, she intended to let her new friend and confidant teach her the skills. But beyond cooking skills, she wasn't ready to make any decisions.

Well, all except one. When Sierra returned to the base, she fully intended to put in for a place of her own. Even if it meant moving off base. After having her own quarters for her and Rhaegar, there was no way she'd return to the barracks. And there was no way she'd give up the search for her best friend, just like Rhaegar never gave up on her.

Sierra arrived at the VA hospital and checked in. Not one to sit idle, she pulled out her phone, deciding to make use of her time while waiting for her appointment with Dr. Alfonzo.

"Sergeant Michaels." The clipped voice that answered her call was anything but warm.

"Hi. This is Sergeant Sierra Winters. Again. I hate to keep bothering you, but I'm wondering if you've heard anything about Rhaegar? My dog," she added, trying to jog the man's memory.

"Sorry, nothing yet, ma'am. I did confirm the dog is back in the U.S. The paperwork shows he left Afghanistan by aircraft carrier. But there are some issues, and we can't tell where he was sent or who picked him up. I'm trying to track things back to the clinic in Afghanistan and see if they can tell us anything. These things take time." It sounded more like yadda, yadda, yadda rhetoric.

It had already been over three weeks. How much time did they need? "I understand. Thanks for your efforts. I'll check back in a couple of days if I don't hear from you." She didn't understand but arguing would get her nowhere and end the search. Rhaegar had been discharged, and she was a sergeant, not high enough on the military totem pole to garner special attention. She needed to appreciate any efforts the other sergeant made, at least vocally, even if it's not how she felt inside.

"I will call you if I learn anything, ma'am. I've got all your information."

"I know. But Rhaegar is my family. We were a team. Best friends. And every day without him, not knowing how he's really doing is tearing me apart inside." It was the closest she'd come to begging for anything in her life. The bond between her and Rhaegar was more than a regular friendship, but she wasn't about to tell a stranger on the phone. Rhaegar had pulled her back to safety just as the bomb had gone off, more than likely saving her life. And that had allowed her to help others to safety. She owed him her life and the lives of others. Rhaegar had been injured in the process, and Sierra needed to know he was okay, and to take care of him much the same way he'd taken care of her.

"I'll do what I can, Sergeant Winters."

"Thanks." She hung up with a heavy heart, her worry growing heavier with each passing day that she might not see her beloved canine friend again. The thought was unsettling.

"Sergeant Sierra Winters," a nurse called out from the door leading into the clinic offices.

She stood and crossed the room. "I'm Sierra Winters."

"Come right this way. Dr. Alfonzo is running a bit behind, but the nurse will be in shortly to talk to you and get some information." She led Sierra down the hall, stopping at one of the rooms. "It looks like you're here to get a calf wound checked out. Is that correct?"

"Yes. There are other shrapnel scars, but they aren't my concern. Just the one that's not playing nice."

"Then you're in luck if it's limited to your calf. We only need you to put on these fancy shorts for the examination." The woman held up an oversized pair of blue paper, disposable shorts and smiled.

"Works for me. I've worn more than enough hospital gowns over the past few months to last me a lifetime." Sierra already hated being here, much less having to strip down. It always made her feel vulnerable.

"If I had a dime for every time I heard that, I'd be rich. I don't know why they can't find a way to make them look nicer." The woman shook her head and laughed as she left the room.

Sierra stripped off her pants and pulled on the shorts, trying to flatten them before sitting down to wait. Her gaze landed on the hideous scar, and she looked away. Vanity wasn't the problem. It was just downright awful to look at. And if she couldn't bear it, she could only imagine how others would react. It warranted consideration when she decided where to live in the future. She'd pick a cold place where shorts weren't worn—ever. Maybe Alaska.

She pulled out her phone and began checking emails. Anything to while away the wait. Sierra heard someone outside her door, which came as a surprise, considering she hadn't been there long.

Shoving the phone back in her pocket, she looked up to greet the doctor.

Noah. What is he doing here?

"It's nice to see you took my advice, Sierra." Noah smiled and crossed the room to the sink to wash his hands.

"Please tell me you weren't serious. That you're not a nurse. More specifically, that you're not *my* nurse." Sierra closed her eyes, wishing for a rock she could crawl under and disappear.

"I can't tell you any of that." He grinned and crossed the room to her side. "Nurse Noah at your service," he said, mocking her use of the name she'd called him yesterday.

"Why do I feel like the world is against me?" A better thought would be when would things go right, but with Noah standing six inches away, and her dressed in funky, unflattering shorts, and her bare legs, it was hard to think positive. "It's a good thing I didn't have to get undressed."

"I could always see about getting that changed," he said, his teasing wink and grin taking the edge off the situation.

"You could, but it wouldn't do any good. I don't take orders from you. These shorts and my legs are bad enough."

"I disagree about the orders. You are here, aren't you?" Noah chuckled, forcing her to face the fact she'd come here on his advice.

The man was odious. "It was suggested, not ordered," she reminded him, trying to maintain a reasonable amount of control over the situation.

"I'll have to remember that in the future." His grin grew wider, the corners of his eyes crinkling. He was enjoying this far too much. "Sit back and let me look at the wound. It's good that you got me because I've seen it recently and can tell if it's gotten worse or better in the last twenty-four hours. And don't worry about the shorts, I see twenty pairs of legs every day, one more pair is no big deal. And honestly, yours are quite nice." Now she knew he was full of bull.

Sierra watched as Noah inspected the wound, his fingertips assessing the skin around the edges. "Does my touch hurt at all? I don't feel any warmth, which is good."

"No, you're fine. I thought you were joking, you know. About the whole nurse thing."

"I get that a lot. Most people think it's a big joke. I happen to love my job. I wanted to make a difference in people's lives. If I'd become a doctor, there'd be less chance to do that on a more personal level. The demands of the job wouldn't allow me time to spend getting to know patients. I get that time as a nurse."

Noah didn't have the same self-esteem issues she suffered from. Her respect for him grew stronger, and again, it wasn't for anything he'd done. It was Noah being Noah.

"I won't tease you about the whole nurse thing if you agree not to mollycoddle me at home anymore. I mean, at your house. *Ugh.* You know what I mean. While I'm staying with your family. And no doctoring outside of this hospital. This is a private matter, and I don't wish it to be discussed at the house."

"You have yourself a deal." Noah shook her hand, his warmth radiating up her arm even in the cold room. "I'm going to be working late tonight, so I probably won't see you until tomorrow. I'll update the doctor with my findings, and he should be in shortly." He headed for the door.

"Noah...thanks. For everything." Turns out, Nurse Noah was a truly nice guy.

The kind who made a girl's heart go pitter-patter if he so much as glanced at her and Sierra was finding she was no exception. Not that it would ever amount to anything. And with Tank as her friend, she'd do well to keep him from suspecting her interest, or she'd never live down the teasing. Or worse, the mortification if Tank told his brother.

However, the bigger problem was Noah Jackson was the first man she'd met who seemed secure enough in himself not to be intimidated by a strong woman. Which in Sierra's books, made him the strongest man she'd ever met, and therefore, the first man she was interested in.

Chapter Seven

♥

NOAH ARRIVED HOME AFTER a long day at the hospital. Leaving a little early, he hoped to be able to see Kaylee and read her a bedtime story before she went to sleep. Walking into the house and seeing no one, he made his way to the kitchen, his stomach in full rumble mode after having missed dinner.

"Hey, Mom," he said, spying her at the sink doing dishes.

"Glad you're home. Kaylee's in the shower. She was hoping you'd be here before bedtime. And, yes, the door is cracked open in case she calls out for me, and I just checked on her." His mother answered the question that immediately popped into his head before he could ask it, putting him at ease.

"Great. Where's Tank and Sierra?"

"I haven't seen either one since dinner. I'm guessing they're out at the barn." She shrugged and turned back to rinse the plate in her hand.

"Okay. I don't need them. I was only curious." Noah couldn't help the twinge of jealousy that struck him. Sierra wasn't Tank's type, as far as he could tell, but then his brother had many types. Having served together, the two of them probably had more in common than Noah wanted to admit.

"How did work go today?" his mother asked. "Did you know Sierra went to the Veteran's hospital? She didn't say much when she got home other than her appointment went well."

Noah remembered his promise to Sierra just in time. "It was a long day. That's great she took me up on my advice. And I'm glad it went well for her." He avoided answering his mother's other question directly because lying wasn't his thing, no matter how great or small the lie.

Sierra had been in more pain today then she cared to admit. He was relieved he'd have the chance to observe her going forward, now knowing all the details of what happened. She'd been through a lot with the surgeries, and her injuries were significant. It was a testament to her strength that she'd rehabbed as far as she had already, but based on his conversation with the doctor, they both agreed she was pushing too hard. It was one thing to keep moving forward to heal, another to overdo it.

Noah wolfed down the plate of leftovers his mother had left in the refrigerator while his daughter finished her shower. "Thanks for dinner. I'm going to check on Kaylee."

"Okay. Her pajamas are laid out on the bathroom counter."

He headed down the hall, the sound of Kaylee laughing and splashing in the shower reaching his ears well before he was halfway there. "I'm home," Noah called out, smiling as he pushed open the bathroom door.

"Daddy!" Kaylie cried out, her face wreathed in smiles as she peeked around the shower curtain. "Look. I washed Barbie's hair, and now it's all clean. I've got to blow-dry it when I get out. I'm gonna make her pretty."

"That will be quite an accomplishment." Noah grinned. The poor doll's hair was stringy and sticking out in all sorts of weird directions. Clearly, the doll wasn't a hairdresser Barbie. "I just wanted to let you know I was home. You've got twenty minutes before bedtime, so perhaps you should wrap it up in here. Here's your towel," he offered, laying it on the closed toilet seat and within reach, "and your pajamas are right here on the counter." He unfolded them to make it easier for her to get dressed. "When you're ready for bed, let me know, and I'll come tuck you in and read you a bedtime story." Noah loved the quiet moments with his daughter at the end of a long day.

"Okay, Daddy. I already picked out the book I want you to read. Grandma got me one of those *Chicken Soup for the Kid's Soul* books, and there are lots of little stories. I love happy endings."

"So do I, honey." Too bad life wasn't always one big happily ever after. But at seven, the reality was not something his daughter needed another dose of.

Noah went into their shared bedroom and got out the clothes he would need for tonight because he didn't like to disturb Kaylee after she had already gone to sleep. Glancing around the room, he let out a deep sigh. Toys were everywhere. He started to pick up the mess, knowing he'd have to have another chat with Kaylee about one toy at a time.

He turned back the bedcovers for her and then looked for her monkey. He was surprised he hadn't found it amongst all the toys on the floor and looked around once again in case he'd missed it. Kaylee never went to bed without her favorite stuffed animal.

Mr. Snuggles was nowhere to be found, and Noah headed back toward the living room to search. Not seeing it, he entered the kitchen just as his mother was taking off her apron, finished for the night.

"Mom, have you seen Mr. Snuggles? I've checked everywhere in Kaylee's room and in the living room, and I can't find it. I hope she didn't take it outside, because it's getting dark, and it might be difficult to locate. And you know what happened the last time we couldn't find him." It hadn't been fun for anyone in the house, and it was not something he was looking to repeat.

"Oh boy, yes, I do remember. We all spent an hour searching while Kaylee was in tears. I'll look around behind you. Have you checked your old room? I heard her in there earlier talking with

Sierra. Maybe she left it there." His mother started lifting pillows and cushions. When it came to child's play, one never knew what to expect.

"That sounds like a good possibility, and I'll get right on it. Kaylee's getting out of the shower and is almost ready for bed. Fingers crossed that's where I find it." Noah turned around and headed back down the hall. He didn't have time to run to the barn and ask Sierra to go in his old room. It might have been a nice gesture, but it did seem odd. It was his room, after all.

He pushed open the door, and the hallway light cast a glow toward the bed. Reaching for the light switch, his hand froze in mid-air as he spotted Sierra asleep on the bed. He stepped off to one side to get a better look. Mr. Snuggles was firmly entrenched in her arms, a peaceful look on Sierra's face.

Noah didn't have the heart to take the monkey from her, but then dealing with Kaylee would be worse. He reached for the stuffed animal, but paused just long enough to rethink the action, before pulling his hand back. It was odd that Sierra would be sleeping with a toy clutched to her chest, and it made his heart ache for whatever it was she was going through that she was unwilling to share with others. He wanted to help her, but you couldn't help someone if they wouldn't let you.

He couldn't do it. At least, not until he talked to Kaylee. Maybe there was a way to convince his daughter to share Mr. Snuggles for one night. He backed out of the room and closed the door gently.

Kaylee was coming out of the bathroom and gave him an odd look. "Is something wrong with Sierra, Daddy?"

He shook his head. "No, honey. Everything's fine, but I need to talk to you about something."

"I'm guessing you saw my messy room. I'm sorry. I meant to clean it up, but then I had to eat dinner, and have a bath and—"

"It's not that, honey. I mean, it is that, and you need to do better. But I have something more important I wanted to ask you about." Noah sat down on her bed and patted the place beside him. His daughter moved to sit there, gazing up at him with curious eyes.

"What is it, Daddy?"

"Well, I was looking for Mr. Snuggles, and it turns out he's in my old room—with Sierra. She's sleeping with it. Would you mind very much if we let her sleep with Mr. Snuggles tonight?" He steeled himself for his daughter's reaction.

"Of course not. I'm not a baby. I like having Mr. Snuggles, but I can share. I like Miss Sierra a lot. Besides, I gave him to her to sleep with tonight." Nothing else his daughter might have said in that moment could've shocked him more.

"You did?" Noah couldn't imagine what had prompted his daughter to give up her stuffed animal, but whatever it was, it had to be a good reason. One he wanted to know.

"I was talking with Miss Sierra after dinner. I know I'm not supposed to bother her, but I heard crying coming from your room. I went in to talk to her and wanted to make her feel better." Kaylee looked up at him with worry in her eyes.

The thought of Sierra crying made his heart ache a little bit more. "It's okay, honey. I know we talked about not bothering people but comforting someone is different. I think it was extremely sweet of you. Do you know why she was crying?" Noah was stepping over all sorts of lines trying to get information from his daughter, but he couldn't help it. His worry for Sierra had grown to a point where he couldn't ignore it.

And where was Bruce during all this? His brother didn't seem to be much help when it came to helping his friend. His mother had thought Sierra was out in the barn, but she'd slipped inside to nurse her wounds and hide her pain from everyone. Everyone except Kaylee that is.

"She said her leg was bothering her. But I think she's missing her doggy a lot." Kaylee frowned as if she had the weight of the world on her shoulders.

"What makes you say that?" Noah frowned.

Kaylee shrugged. "I don't know. I mean, she was looking at a picture of him when I went into the room. And she showed it to me. He's a really huge dog."

"You're probably right about her missing him. I'm proud of you for sharing Mr. Snuggles." There was a lot more going on, but he'd save the questions for Sierra, instead of trying to involve his daughter.

"I told her she could sleep with him till she finds Rhaegar."

"You're a pretty special daughter, you know that? It's very grown-up of you to do such a warm and wonderful thing for someone. I think you get a pass on your room. A big heart trumps scattered toys any day of the week." He chuckled. "Now, why don't you hop into bed, and I'll read you the story you wanted."

"That sounds perfect, Daddy. I love you." Kaylee scrambled under the covers, fluffing the pillow the exact way she liked.

"I love you, too, sweetheart." Noah kissed the top of her head and lay back against the pillow he'd grabbed off his bed to lie close together while he read the book. The story was short, but Kaylee's ability to stay awake was even shorter.

Noah slid off the bed, placed the book on the nightstand, and gazed down at his daughter. His heart swelled with love. Brushing back a lock of hair from her cheek, he leaned down to kiss her forehead.

He left the room, leaving the door partly open. He only got as far as the end of the hall, stopping when he heard a strange sound coming from his old room. It sounded like the cry of a wounded animal.

Sierra.

Protocol went out the window as he rushed back down the hall. He had to help her, whether she wanted it or not. Sierra could be angry with him all she wanted come morning, but he wasn't walking away.

Noah moved to the side of the bed and sat down, each one of her whimpering cries slicing his heart into a dozen pieces. He didn't want to frighten her, so he reached out to gently lay a hand on her shoulder, hoping to calm her. "Sierra, wake up. It's me, Noah. Sierra," he repeated, keeping his voice low as he tried to reach her.

She bolted upright, clutching the covers, the fear in her eyes evident even in the dim lighting. "Go away," she cried, trying to pull away from Noah.

"I will once I know you're okay. You were having a bad go of it. Want to tell me what happened?" Talking was the best cure-all for situations like this one. It exposed fear to the light and was a big step to eradicating it.

"No. Not really. It's nothing," Sierra said, her lower lip quivering.

"Hardly nothing, given what I heard. It helps to talk about these things. Trust me." Somehow, Noah needed to find a way to get her talking. Judging by what he'd witnessed, Sierra had a lot further to go in the healing process than he'd originally suspected. *Mental healing.*

"Talking just makes a person remember more. I think it's highly overrated." Noah noticed she still hadn't let go of Mr. Snuggles. It was the one shred of comfort she'd accepted so far, and he wouldn't mention it, knowing she'd hate that he'd seen any weakness.

"Try me because whatever you've been doing so far isn't working. It's been almost three months."

Sierra stopped pulling away. "You're a nurse, not a shrink."

"I'm a good listener." The tension eased in her shoulders, and her eyes no longer held dark fear. No matter what she said, he was making progress and would stay the course.

"You're not going away until I tell you, are you?" She shook her head, letting out a deep sigh.

Noah smiled, trying to reassure her. "Nope. Consider it my duty. Not as your doctor, but as your friend."

"Nurse," she countered, a half-smile on her face.

Progress in his books. "Splitting hairs. It's the friend part that counts."

"Conditioner takes care of split ends. Maybe a good shower will wash you right out of the room." Her dimples deepened as she fought off what he felt would have been a much bigger smile.

"Quit stalling," he said, pleased they were operating on level ground now.

"Fine. If it makes you leave, I'll tell you. But remember, you promised me privacy regarding anything about my health or my state of mind." Her focused gaze waited for him to confirm before she continued.

Noah nodded, giving her the reassurance she needed.

"I think I have PTSD." It wasn't news to him, but judging by the way Sierra said it, it was the last thing she wanted to admit.

"Understandable, given what you've been through. Tell me what happens," Noah urged her to continue.

"How would you know?" Her brow pulled tightly as she watched him.

"Don't you ever talk to Tank? I mean, really talk?" He would have thought the two of them would have discussed what happened given they'd been through it together.

"We talk all the time." Sierra crossed her arms in front of her, nuzzling her chin into the monkey's head.

"Clearly not about what's important. Bruce has PTSD, too, in case you haven't guessed. Not that he'll talk to me about it. The two of you could help each other. It's nothing to be ashamed of or hide. People in war see horrible things. They can be dealt with, but only if you want help."

"I think you should become a shrink." Sierra tried to joke about the situation, but this wasn't a laughing matter.

"Why is that? Just because I'm stating the obvious. I work with active-duty soldiers and veterans all the time. You're not the first person I've dealt with that has this condition, and you certainly won't be the last." Each case was different with varying degrees of healing. There was no tried or true method to make things right, but they all had one thing in common—the need to start somewhere—usually by talking.

"But what if I don't want it?" she asked, her voice quivering.

Noah reached out to take her hand. "Then it's up to you to work through this and work toward healing. And I'll be right here for you."

"Okay, fine. But I don't want to talk about it anymore right now. Give me a little more time. And thanks for telling me about Tank. I didn't realize." Her eyes darkened with concern, a true testament to how much she cared about Bruce.

"He hides it well, but I'm his brother. I notice things. Just like I notice them about you." It was the truth. He noticed everything about her, whether he should or not.

"Maybe you should stop looking," she said, one eyebrow cocked upward.

"Fat chance." He grinned, his words meaning far more to him than to her, but what she didn't know, certainly wouldn't hurt in this case. Noah headed for the door, recognizing it wouldn't do any good to push her harder. She'd already opened the door, and now that he had his foot in it, he wouldn't let her close it again.

Chapter Eight

♥

THE NEXT MORNING, SIERRA brushed the sleep from her eyes, her gaze landing on the monkey in bed with her.

Noah. Images of last night came rushing back to greet her like a long-lost archenemy. Not remembering would be better. She lay back down, groaning. "Why me? God, haven't I been through enough? Now you want to add humiliation to the mix?"

Sierra pulled the covers over her head, blocking out the light. Minutes passed, but nothing changed. Running away from the issue wouldn't solve anything. Never had. Never would. She pushed back the covers, forced herself out of bed, and limped her way to the bathroom without her crutch. As luck would have it, Noah was just coming out. That's what she called bad luck.

"Good morning, Sierra. Feeling any better?" His husky morning voice slid down her spine. Warm and comforting like a blanket.

"I do. I, *ummm...* Sorry about last night. I think the pain pills were a little more than I'm used to." She latched on to the first good excuse she could find.

"I noticed the doctor upped your prescription. Hopefully, it takes the edge off, and you won't limp as much. That makes everything worse. Next thing you know, it'll be your hips and your feet adding pain to the mix." Noah had gone into nurse mode on her, but for once, she didn't mind his molly-coddling, preferring to think of it as him being protective.

"That's what everyone keeps telling me, but I let the pain and inflammation get away from me this time. Are you finished here?" she asked, pointing at the bathroom. The man had a way of drawing her out of her comfort zone. Like sneaking up on her. The fact she didn't mind was more than a bit concerning.

"I am." He smiled, making room for her to enter. "Sierra, about last night..."

"Forget last night. Please." It would be better for them both if he did. She wasn't used to opening to anyone and spilling her guts, and this morning, the thought of retreating from the closeness they'd established looked pretty darn good. Her own personal darkness was better than sharing her fears and weaknesses and bringing them into the light.

Noah shook his head. "I can't forget about it. But know that I'm here for you if you need me. And remember, you promised to talk to Bruce."

"I don't recall that promise, but I'll try." Talking to Tank would mean allowing another human to see into her soul. But what if Noah was right and Tank needed help. Sierra wouldn't turn her back on a friend, no matter how much it hurt her in the process.

Noah saluted and turned to walk away. In the military, a salute was a sign of respect. Sierra couldn't help but wonder how Noah meant the gesture. Sarcasm or respect? She was betting on sarcasm because she kept shutting him out. Not to mention, she'd done nothing to earn his respect.

After a quick shower, she headed for the kitchen, feeling more refreshed and ready to face the day. "Good morning, Laura," she said, finding the woman already fixing breakfast.

"Good morning, dear. I hope you slept well." The simple question reassured her Noah had kept his promise and remained silent about their discussion.

"I did." It was a lie, but she wasn't going unburden her soul to Laura. The woman had enough on her plate without Sierra adding to it and making her worry. "Where is everyone?"

Kaylee came charging through the back door. "Is breakfast ready? I'm starved."

"Sure is. Go wash up." Laura was good with the girl, the love in her eyes obvious every time she spotted her granddaughter.

"Good morning, Miss Sierra. Did Mr. Snuggles make you feel better last night?"

Sierra winced, shooting a sharp glance at Laura, hoping she hadn't heard the comment. No such luck. "He certainly did. Thank you so much for sharing him." It was the truth.

"Goody. I'll be right back." Kaylee tore out of the room as fast as she had entered.

"That child has more energy in her pinky than I have in my body." Laura laughed. "Noah left for work already, but Bruce is out in the barn. Any chance you can go over there and call him in for breakfast?"

"No problem. Anything I can do to help would be a blessing, considering I'm useless at doing chores around the ranch." It still rankled she couldn't help, but she didn't dare test Noah on the matter. Not to mention, she did need to let her leg heal if she would have any chance of returning to active duty in a month.

"*Tsk-tsk.* You're not useless. It's all a matter of finding ways you can help. Let me think on it a bit and see what I come up with."

"Thanks. That would be great." Sierra meant it, but she wasn't sure there was anything Laura could think of. Or at least, not something Sierra would enjoy doing. She liked hard, challenging work and being outdoors. Those were the kinds of things that had her name on them—all things she couldn't do at this point.

She headed out the door, intent on finding Tank. Her feet dragged a bit, but not because they were hurting. More because Noah's words were still echoing in her head, and she wasn't sure what to say to her friend.

Why wouldn't Tank have said anything to her? Probably for the same reason she hadn't talked to him. Who wanted to admit to weakness? Sierra already dealt with the curious gazes and sympathetic looks of others. How much worse would it be if they discovered she had PTSD? Her plan of action was to give it time. Time healed all wounds, at least that's what people said.

But what if Noah was right? Sierra was the one who'd chosen the path they'd taken that fateful day. She owed it to her friend to make sure he was okay.

"Tank?" she called out.

"Up here," he answered from the loft, peering down over the edge.

"Breakfast will be ready in a few minutes. Your mother sent me to get you." She stood there, hands on hips, and waited for him to join her, determined to take advantage of the privacy.

"Okay. I just need to finish cleaning this last section, and I'll be there."

Her stomach clenched. "I was hoping we'd get a few minutes to talk. We haven't had much time alone since I got here." She scuffed her boot against some strands of hay that littered the floor.

He popped his head back over the side, a frown etched on his face. "What did you want to talk about?"

"About what happened. You know, overseas." She forced the words out between her lips, opening the conversation like a can of scorpions.

He shook his head. "*Awww*, Sierra, I know you don't like to talk about it. And neither do I. It's in the past."

"Tank, please, come down," she insisted, unwilling to give up easily now that she'd started down this road.

He paused only a minute before descending the ladder, but not before she'd seen a look of resignation on his face. "What?" he asked, pulling off his gloves and tossing them on the crate nearby.

"Why can't we talk about it? I've been thinking it might do me some good. Do *us* some good." Putting herself on the line was the bait to make him talk. If she so much as hinted it was only for him, he'd shut down tighter than a clam.

"What gives you the idea I need to talk about it? I'm fine." Tank shrugged. "If you need someone—"

"Your brother thinks otherwise," she interjected, not willing to let him slide out of the conversation easily. She wouldn't go down this road alone, not since she was doing it for Tank.

He glared at her. "My brother has a big mouth."

Sierra rolled her eyes. "He's a nurse. What do you expect? He can't ignore what he sees and act like it doesn't exist." Noah had been the same way with her since they'd met. It was in his nature to care for others.

Tank propped his booted foot up on a crate and looked at her as if she'd lost her mind. "As if I'd take advice from a nurse." Sierra was more than a little surprised at the disdain in his voice.

"There's nothing wrong with his career choice. He loves his job. And attacking him or his talents won't change things for you." Sierra took the bull by the horns and held on tight.

"Defending my brother? Whose friend are you anyway?" This bull was more like a military tank, making his nickname more than appropriate. That was exactly why he'd been stuck with it when he first enlisted. The guy was more bullheaded than any other private she'd come across in her ten years in the military.

"Both. Look, I have nightmares. We both know what happened is my fault, but I can't change it. I need your forgiveness if I'm going to have any chance of moving past this. I need to know the guys don't blame me." She hadn't thought of it until now, but it was the truth. All her time in church as a youngster had taught her that forgiveness was the first step to fixing a problem.

Tank's eyes shot wide open, his brow drawn tight. "What are you talking about? It wasn't your fault. You didn't put the bomb there, and there was no way for you to know. None of the guys think you're responsible for what happened."

She'd tried to convince herself of that over and over but to no avail. "There's not a minute that goes by that I don't wish I'd chosen differently. I failed the team."

"Every one of us was serving our country by choice, Sierra. We risked our lives for a purpose.

Don't rob us of that by taking the blame. The enemy is responsible, but that's where the line is drawn." Tank was serious.

"*Ouch.* For a man who didn't want to talk, you have a lot to say." She frowned, his words making sense and trying to take over her brain. Still, the dark corners resisted the light. There was a tiny doubt that said he was wrong.

"You want the truth? Sure, I have nightmares. Satisfied? But I don't blame you. If it hadn't been for you and Rhaegar, we would all be dead." Tank ran his hands through his hair, struggling with his admission.

"No, I'm not satisfied." She would never be satisfied with the result knowing Robert Brady's family were suffering.

"Who's to say the other route wouldn't have been worse?" It was the same question she'd asked herself a million times.

"It's something I'll never know. One life lost is too many, and I have to live with the consequences of my decision."

"Sounds to me like you need to focus on the positives. You're in a no-win game with your head if you don't change your way of thinking. I thought you were smarter than this."

"Then help me. I want us to help each other out. As equals." She reached for his arm, needing to connect with him as the rush of memories assailed her. "As friends," she added.

Tank looked like he wanted to argue, but suddenly, the tension left his body as he let out a deep breath. "The truth is, I don't know what to do. The images pop in from out of nowhere. A sound here. A sound there. Anything can set them off. That's why I'm out here all the time. Alone. It's better this way."

"I understand. I was trying to do the same thing, but there was nowhere to run and hide at home. And my father had plenty to say on the matter. Trust me, he disagrees with you on the blame game." Even after ten years of service, her father hadn't accepted that his daughter was in the military. Too many times, she'd heard him mention his view on women in the service, and she'd done nothing but prove him right.

Tank frowned. "Your father wasn't there. What would he know?"

"Don't forget, he's a retired colonel. Need I say more? Trust me, for a guy who wasn't there, he has a lot to say." Sierra cracked a smile.

"Then it's a good thing you came here. And you're welcome to stay until you report back to duty. No one needs that kind of baloney heaped on them after what we've been through," Tank said, his voice taking on a defensive tone.

"I'm glad I came here, and I really appreciated the invitation. You had my back...just like always." It was like having two brothers, the Jackson boys always at the ready to defend her. Only one of them didn't elicit brotherly love—even more reason to avoid Noah.

"Anytime, pip-squeak." He bumped her shoulder teasingly as they headed out of the barn.

She stopped, hands on hips, and glared at him. "What? Pip-squeak? I don't like that at all."

Tank grinned. "Of course, you don't. But it's what I wanted to call you the whole time we served together, but I couldn't because you outranked me. No such problem now," he said, taking a few steps to separate them and stay out of her reach.

"Take it back," she fumed, stepping closer.

"Or what?"

"Or I'll... I'll beat you with my cane." Sierra held up her weapon and suddenly burst out laughing at the expression on Tank's face.

"A terrifying pip-squeak...is that better?" He grinned, taking another step back in retreat.

Sierra's stomach rumbled, a reminder of where they were supposed to be. "Much. We better get a move on, or your mother will have our hides."

"That's true. And, Sierra, thanks. I appreciate what you're trying to do for both of us. And for that reason, I'll try, too. Maybe talking to each other about it will help. At least we both understand." Tank took her hand and squeezed it.

They were comrades again, just not in arms.

Over breakfast it was as though nothing had happened between the two of them. Kaylee went on and on, filling any void in the conversation.

"Miss Sierra, will you help me pick out my school clothes? Daddy laid out an outfit, but it's not very princess like. I'm sure you're way better at it." Kaylee beamed up at her like she was some magical fashion fairy about to come to her rescue.

"I don't know about that. I'm a jeans-and-T-shirt kind of person." She always had been, much to her father's consternation.

"But you could try." Kaylee pouted, not for a minute willing to give up on the request.

It was impossible to resist her plea. If only Kaylee knew what she was getting herself into. "Okay, but don't blame me if it looks more spinsterish than a princess."

Kaylee scrunched up her face. "What's spintish mean?"

"Spinsterish. Old lady-like." Sierra couldn't help but grin as she set the little girl straight.

"But why would you want me to look like an old lady?" Kaylee asked in all innocence.

Tank coughed, but Sierra caught the grin he was hiding. "What she means is the clothes might not match the way you want them, too, Kaylee. Not that she would intentionally make you look old."

Kaylee shook her head and frowned. "Grown-ups. I can't understand you all sometimes. If I'm going to have to pick out my own clothes, then can you help me with my hair? Daddy didn't do it this morning."

"Kaylee, let Sierra eat her breakfast. You know I fix your hair in the mornings." Laura's answer had let Sierra off the hook because she didn't know any response that would get her out of the new request without hurting the girl's feelings.

"Don't you like me?" Kaylee turned big blue eyes on her.

"Why would you ask that? Of course, I like you."

"You don't want to do things with me—like mommy things. You know mine's not here, and I need someone. I mean, Grandma helps me, but it's not the same." She cast an apologetic look at her grandmother.

Sierra was glad Noah wasn't here for this conversation.

"Kaylee, that's not—" Laura started to say.

"It's okay, let me answer." Sierra nodded her head to reassure the woman. "Honey, it's not that I don't like you. What's not to like? You have a big heart and helped me out so much yesterday. I'll forever be indebted to you for sharing Mr. Snuggles." The others were listening, but she ignored their curious stares. This was about Kaylee. For the second time today, she found herself not caring what others thought of her, and more concerned with helping.

"I'm not good at girl stuff because I liked to do boy things when I was a child. I used to get dirty in the mud. Play army. Wrestle. I wasn't into pretty dresses and fixing my hair the way you are. Not that my father didn't want me to be, mind you." In fact, her father's attitude and him telling her she couldn't do things like a rambunctious boy had made her even more deter- mined to do them. The little plastic army men in a shoebox under her bed were a perfect rebellion.

"*Hmmm*. Then I have a great idea, why don't we learn together. Then your daddy will be so proud of you."

"Sure thing, honey." Sierra smiled, reassuring the girl, at least for the moment. There was no way she would hurt Kaylee and Sierra's experience when it came to parenting a child amounted to zero. But it hadn't stopped Kaylee from forming an attachment with her, something Sierra hoped would end well when she left.

"Bruce, can you run Kaylee to school today? I've got something I want to talk to Sierra about," Laura asked as she started to clear the table.

"No problem. Especially as it gets me out of doing the dishes." Tank stood and headed for the door. "Go wash up, kiddo. Almost time to go."

"Okay," Kaylee chimed. She ran around the table and stopped to give Sierra a hug. "I'm glad you're here. We're going to have so much fun together. Bye, Grandma." And with that, she turned and skipped out of the room.

"Sounds like you have an admirer." Tank glanced her way and grinned.

"Don't tell Noah. I wouldn't want to worry him. He's quite protective." Total understatement.

Laura scoffed. "There's nothing wrong with a child's adoration. I'll deal with Noah when he figures it out."

"Nicely said, Mother." Tank dropped a kiss on her cheek and left.

"What did you want to talk about?" Sierra asked, rising to help clear the table.

"I thought about what you can do, given your injury and that you're trying to recuperate," Laura said, a smile lighting her face. "It's perfect if you ask me."

Sierra stopped at the sink, anxious to hear what Laura had in mind. "What's that?"

"There's a ranch just up the road from here called Whispering Pines. A retired pro bull rider owns it, and he set up a volunteer program called the GiddyUp Kids. They've been asking around town for volunteers, and I'm thinking it might be a good fit for you. It's walking and riding horses." Laura beamed, pleased she'd found something that sounded like it would work.

Sierra wasn't so sure. "I don't know. It's been a while since I've been on a horse." And then there was the more obvious issue of her leg.

"It wouldn't be nearly as strenuous as farm work, and it would be way more fulfilling. Exercise and fresh air without strain. Therefore perfect."

Laura was right about that part. Not to mention, if she didn't do something with her time, she'd find herself playing mommy to Kaylee whether she wanted to or not. And no matter what Laura said, Sierra didn't want to do that. She didn't have the first clue how to act in a mommy role, and more importantly, Noah would have a thing or two to say. And they wouldn't be good things.

She could at least check out the gig at Whispering Pines. Otherwise, it was time to return home, and she wasn't ready for that, either. The one bright side of the deal was that her stupid leg should be less of an issue on a horse. The more she thought about it, the more she liked the idea. And she wasn't one to back down from trying anything. "I'll do it. Or at least go talk to the guy."

"Wonderful. I'll let Chad Andrews know you're coming. Nice guy and newly married."

"Let's hope he's as positive I can do this as you are." Sierra took the paper Laura handed her, mentally noting the address before shoving it in her back pocket. Right after the dishes were done, she'd head on over to the Whispering Pines Ranch.

What did she have to lose besides the rest of her dignity if this Chad guy didn't want her? Or worse, what if he did take her on, and then she failed?

Sierra followed the directions Laura had written down for her. It wasn't long before she was turning onto a gravel road and passing under a wrought-iron archway over the driveway that indicated she was in the right place. *Whispering Pines.*

The wooded area on both sides was blanketed in an array of brilliant red, orange, and yellow. The leaves were beautiful this time of year. People traveled from all over to come to view the splendor of a New England fall, hoping to catch the spectacular show.

Nothing had prepared Sierra for the beauty of the majestic log home at the top of the hill. The name Chad Andrews rang a bell, but her dad hadn't let her go to rodeos as a child. Only tea parties and dances were right for his little girl. Sierra cringed at the memory of being forced into a dress and paraded around like a doll.

She grabbed her cane and exited the car, stopping to gaze at the pasture where horses were grazing. A picturesque setting of tranquility, and one she'd love to lose herself in if possible. This was a place where all the cares and worries of the world disappeared.

"Peaceful, isn't it?" A man's voice startled her, and she turned to see who it was. Her first guess was Chad Andrews himself—the guy every inch a cowboy. Older, but still in great shape, someone with confidence she suspected came from mastering a bull in the ring. Talk about insanity.

Sierra smiled. "It is. I can't imagine waking up to this view each day. Or ever wanting to leave."

"Wait till you see the view out back." He grinned and stuck out his hand. "Name's Chad Andrews. And I'm guessing you're Sierra Winters?"

"I am. Thanks for meeting with me. Laura Jackson spoke highly of you, but honestly, Mr. Andrews, I'm not sure of what use I can be to you." She'd promised to check things out, and just seeing the place made it worthwhile, but she also knew the reality. It would more than likely be the first and last time she visited.

He gazed at her with interest, his expression not giving away any clue as to what he was thinking. "Chad, please. If we're going to be working together, I prefer being on a first-name basis." He acted as though she hadn't voiced her qualms about the work.

"Okay, Chad, it is. But you know this would only be temporary, right? I've got to report back to the base in early December."

"This is a non-profit organization. Help is always appreciated for as long as you can give it." There was no arguing the point.

Sierra shrugged. "Then why don't you tell me what it is you need help with? As you can tell, my abilities are somewhat limited." The idea of sharing her weakness with a stranger left her reeling.

"Let's take a walk and talk. Just watch your step."

"Of course, canes and fields probably aren't a good mix." He was all but telling her no before they even had a chance to talk. She didn't have to read his expression, his words enough for her to get the message.

"Actually, shoes and manure don't mix." He chuckled. "I'm sure you can manage the rest, or you wouldn't have come in the first place."

"Gotcha. Sorry." She hadn't given him the benefit of the doubt, a mistake she didn't plan on making again. The man was a straight shooter.

"You can come meet the horses and get a feel for the place."

"Okay, lead on." They walked toward the pasture, Chad's pace slow and steady. She appreciated the gesture, but part of her resented the necessity.

"We give riding lessons, but also have a special program called the *GiddyUp Kids*. It helps children with various disabilities have a chance to enjoy things other children do. Because of their limitations, they require extra care and supervision. It's a volunteer program, and the kids come out several times a week. It's grown in popularity, and I don't have the heart to turn down a child in need."

"It sounds awesome. I haven't ridden in ages, and given my current, *ummm*...injury, I'm not sure how good I'll be at it now." After she got back to the Jackson's, she planned on doing a little research on the program and the cowboy who ran it. Chad Andrews was an amazing man with a big heart. A reliable, stand-up kind of guy who put others ahead of himself. A person worthy of her respect, not just because of what he did for others, but also because of the man himself.

A man like Noah.

"Laura told me a little about you. The way I see it, if you love horses and kids, you'll do fine. As for your injury, you're walking. I consider that a blessing and a win. Don't you?"

Sierra hadn't thought of it that way, but he was right. "True."

"The children will actually accept you more readily, seeing you as one of them, even if it's a temporary condition for you. The question is, can you ride? And there's only one way to find out. I've saddled up Sugar for you. My wife, Amy, will be joining us." He pointed toward where a woman stood with three horses.

Sierra wasn't sure she was ready for this. What if she fell off and made a fool of herself? What if it hurt her leg, and she cried like a baby? She could play the what-if game for the rest of the day or suck it up and ride. There was only one choice she could make. "Okay, I'm game." She shrugged, knowing she thrived on challenges, and this was just one more in a long line of challenges her future would bring.

A beautiful woman in her mid-fifties dressed in jeans and a plaid shirt handed her a set of reins. "Hi, I'm Amy Andrews. This is Sugar, and she's a real sweetheart."

"I'm Sierra Winters. It's nice to meet you. It's been a while since I've been on a horse, so bear with me if I'm a little slow on the uptake." A little while was an understatement—more like thirteen years.

"You'll be fine, dear. Riding a horse is like riding a bike. Get on, and it will come back to you." Everyone kept saying the same thing. Now, it was up to Sierra to believe it.

"I promise you, Sugar's an extremely calm and patient mare. We use her with all our first-timers. You'll be safe," Chad said, offering reassurance.

Sierra reached out to touch the mare's nose, stroking down the length of her velvety fuzz. Sugar sniffed her hand and nuzzled it, searching for more attention. Sierra laughed, immediately falling in love with the big, white beast.

"Do you need a hand getting up?" Chad asked. "No, I'm good." Not the smartest answer, but the only one she could give. It wasn't in her to ask for help. Of course, part of her still hated that she might need it.

Sierra crossed to the fence and set her cane against it. She limped her way to the horse and hoisted the foot of her strong leg into the stirrup.

Trying to keep the weight off her injured leg as much as possible, she quickly pushed off and up, tossing her left leg over the saddle, and using her hands on the pommel to brace and assist the move.

Pain rifled down her leg, but not enough to stop her. "Step one, I'm on," she ground out, fighting back against showing any weakness.

"Great. We'll show you the trails and routes we take with the children, so you can see there are no dangers. We keep safety in mind first and foremost," Chad said as Amy started out, leading the way.

"Sounds good." The pain had already started to let up, and Sierra was more than ready to ride. Just being on the back of a horse again felt incredible, as though breathing life into her. It gave her a sense of purpose.

The powerful mare walked along the path without a care, her legs strong and capable. And that's when it hit Sierra—she was riding. The horse was her legs, and she could ride, explore, and move about in ways she hadn't in months. It was easy to understand why the children would love this.

For the next hour they rode, the Andrews couple pointing out special views, wildlife, and the various trails, all while telling tales of the children. When she realized they were back at the barn, she dismounted with a sense of disappointment.

"So, what did you think?" Amy asked as Chad took the reins from Sierra and handed her the cane.

"I loved it. I can't begin to explain how it felt after months of being restricted in everything I do." She felt alive. More alive than she had since the explosion. Even before that, if she was honest with herself.

"Which is exactly what Laura thought would happen when she suggested you'd be perfect," Chad said, coming to stand with them.

"If the offer's still open to help out with the *GiddyUp Kids*, I'd love to accept." Sierra meant every word. This could be a new chapter in her life.

"Absolutely. Like I mentioned earlier, we give lessons and take groups on rides. Any time you want to come out and help is fine with me. I think you'll fit in great."

Sierra was taken aback by the man's sincerity and his genuine offer. Deep-seated emotions she'd been tamping down swirled to the surface. Chad An-drews thought she was good enough. "How about every day, starting tomorrow?"

"I like it. A lot. Welcome aboard, Sierra."

She still had to go home for Thanksgiving but working here would give her an excellent excuse to avoid home until then. Of course, it was contingent on Laura not minding her sticking around a bit longer.

Her father had reminded her of her injury daily and tried to convince her to give up the military life and settle down to get a job in Boston. It was one of the reasons she had to escape her own home. It was her life—not his. She'd toyed with the idea of leaving the military after the attack. Any sane person would rethink their commitment. But it was what she knew and loved, and it was her future by choice. Or it had been until the injury.

She didn't want to think about any of that now, preferring to embrace the new freedom she'd found here.

The future wasn't today, not by a long shot.

Chapter Nine

NOAH WASN'T HAPPY ABOUT Sierra working at Whispering Pines Ranch. Only a couple of days had passed, and her pronounced limp hadn't gone unnoticed. He still couldn't believe his mother had suggested it, but then Sierra had made him promise not to discuss her injury and health issues. He'd honor that promise, but it didn't mean he had to like it.

Taking it easy didn't seem to be a part of Sierra's repertoire, but she seemed happier—more relaxed. Especially around Kaylee and his mom.

Everyone seemed to have forgotten this was a temporary situation, his entire family falling into a daily routine as though Sierra were a permanent fixture in their family. Visitors didn't take jobs, even if it was volunteer work and part-time. Although, based on the amount of time she spent there, it was more like a part-time plus. Kaylee would be crushed when her new best friend waltzed out her life, but how could she not get wrapped up in Sierra when his own mother doted on the woman like a daughter.

The three spent lots of time in the kitchen, Sierra and Kaylee getting cooking lessons. His mother was in her element. It didn't matter that he hadn't wanted Sierra and Kaylee getting close—it happened anyway. His daughter had even chosen to sit between Sierra and his mother at church this morning, sharing her Bible since Sierra didn't have one. It would seem he was the only one who had a problem with the deepening connections, or the end result when Sierra left. Maybe he should come right out and ask her when she was leaving, making sure his daughter was made aware of the information in an attempt to keep her feet and her heart grounded.

Noah liked Sierra, too. But liking her didn't change a thing. He had a responsibility to Kaylee. For that reason, he'd keep any wayward desire to let himself get to know her better on lockdown. Sierra was beautiful, smart, and had a gentle spirit that called out to him. But the problem with trusting his judgment was that he'd thought his first wife, Blanche, was the type of woman he wanted and would make a good wife. Easygoing. Successful. Loved kids.

He couldn't have been more wrong.

After they'd gotten married, he'd discovered she was easygoing with her socialite friends, and successful because she was daddy's spoiled princess. His ex-wife hadn't been liked or respected at her office, and she'd certainly had no interest in having kids. She'd put on a show for the charity fundraisers, and not because of any great love for children. When she'd accidentally gotten pregnant, it had been the beginning of the end. They'd made it five years before she'd given up and returned to the city's bright lights.

If he could be that wrong once, it could happen again, something not worth the risk. Not with Kaylee involved. He'd protect his daughter, at any cost, from getting hurt again the way her mother had hurt her when she deserted the family.

And then there was the issue of Bruce. One didn't poach on a brother's love interest, even if said brother had never been committed to any woman and could only leave a trail of broken hearts. He had yet to see real proof they were involved, but how could they not be?

He needed to just come right out and ask Bruce—or Sierra, for that matter. Trusting his own judgment when it came to women wasn't a good idea based on his record, but there was one person's opinion he could trust—his mother. She'd never connected with Blanche, and rightly so. Sierra was a different story.

"Hey, there. How's the shoeing going?" Bruce asked, running a hand down the mare's flank.

Noah set the horse's leg down and looked up. "It's going. I'm not the fastest at the job, but I'll get it done. Good thing Mabel here doesn't mind and is patient, unlike some of the other horses." Noah grinned. They both knew ranching wasn't his thing. He loved his mother, and for her, he'd help when needed—which was far too often in Noah's opinion. His being here delayed the inevitable of them bringing in the help needed to manage the load.

"Yeah, she is a sweetheart. You hungry? It's getting close to lunch, and I've made substantial progress on today's chores." Bruce stepped back, giving him room to maneuver Mabel toward her stall.

"If my stomach is anything to go by, I'd say the answer is yes. Been rumbling the past twenty minutes." Noah laughed, sliding the handle into place on the gate.

The two men walked side by side and headed for the house. Bruce was more relaxed lately, but still on the quiet side.

"Can I ask you a question?" Noah knew he was about to venture into what was considered forbidden territory, but he couldn't resist.

"Sure. What's up?" His brother's suddenly tense shoulders and slight frown said anything but sure. Noah knew Bruce's time in Afghanistan was off-limits, and he'd always been respectful of that and never pressed Bruce. He'd hoped they were moving past this stage with Sierra in the picture, but given

Bruce's sudden tension, the progress wasn't as advanced as Noah had expected.

"It's about Sierra."

Bruce let out the breath he'd been holding. "What about her? She's great, isn't she?" He grinned and cocked one eyebrow as he glanced at Noah curiously.

"She seems to be. I mean, she's got issues, but I think she's nice," Noah said, soft shoeing to the point.

"Nice? That's an understatement. That woman's all heart and fire, but don't tell her I said that. She wouldn't like the heart part." His brother's grin deepened.

"You have my word." Noah knew from personal experience Sierra would hate the comment, but he wasn't about to tell his brother that, because then Bruce would push to find out how he knew.

"When you mentioned issues, are you referring to her injuries?"

Noah shrugged. "It's more than that, but not what I wanted to talk about." He set Bruce at ease, knowing his brother understood him completely without putting it into so many words.

"Then what do you want to know, and why are you asking me instead of her?" Bruce leveled him with a gaze that said he wouldn't be telling stories on his friend.

Noah didn't want details on Sierra, but the information he wanted was delicate.

"Because you're my brother. Do you like her?" It was always better to come right out and ask.

"Of course. Why would I have invited Sierra here if I didn't?" His brother's brow drew tight in confusion.

It wasn't the answer Noah wanted to hear. "That's what I thought." He let out the deep breath he'd been holding.

"Oh, wait a minute. Are you asking me—" he slapped a hand against his head, "—if I *like* like her?" Bruce's expression was suddenly filled with mirth.

"We're not in sixth grade. Of course, that's what I'm asking." Noah shook his head and rolled his eyes, his brother's slow understanding making it awkward.

Bruce chuckled. "Not in the way you're asking then. I consider us best friends. Besides, I've got a special lady friend in Boston that I *like* like. And the last time we had a conversation like this was when I was in the sixth grade if my memory serves me correctly. Little Jenny Matthews was her name."

"Ha-ha, hilarious, wise guy. How was I to know you liked her? Talk about a far reach," Noah said, playfully pushing against his brother's shoulder.

"What? You don't think I was good enough for her?" Bruce exclaimed with false incredulity.

"No. You were too young. In school, eighth graders didn't go out with sixth graders." The two brothers had never seemed to be on the same page growing up. It was as if Bruce resented that Noah was older and allowed more freedom. It hadn't helped that Noah thought of him as a nuisance trying to hang around all the time. If he could turn back time and change their childhood, that would be the one thing he'd change. Anything to make the relationship he had with his brother today, a stronger one.

"True. But then, neither one of us got to date the girl, so it ended well."

Noah smiled, the memory not one he'd thought of since high school. "How was I to know eighth graders were into tenth-grade football players and not smart guys her own age? So, tell me about your lady friend. We have yet to meet her. Is it serious?" It was the longest his brother had talked about his mystery woman. His reticence to discuss her, was something that had caused Noah to question her existence. Not that he'd verbalize his doubts.

"Why all the... I get it. You like Sierra and want my permission to date her." Bruce clapped him on the shoulder, grinning ear to ear.

"Not at all. It was just curiosity on your behalf. I can't get involved, not with Kaylee in the picture." Speaking the words out loud brought the situation into the light, confirming that his reasoning was sound. Not to mention, he didn't want his brother to get any ideas that couldn't be squashed. At least, not until he knew for sure what to do about the attraction between him and Sierra.

"Hogwash. Quit hiding behind Kaylee and move forward with your life. You can't let Blanche rob you of more happiness than she has already. And Kaylee is a good reason to consider a relationship, not run from them. My niece could use a mother figure. It's not like I don't have eyes to see how she is with Sierra."

His brother's words touched a sensitive chord. "Interesting perspective from a guy who's hiding behind his time serving this country and not moving forward with his life."

Bruce flinched like he'd been slapped.

Noah wanted to kick himself. He'd reacted in self-defense, and it had been the wrong thing to say. "Sorry, I didn't mean to say that."

"Sure, you did. Been skirting around the issue since I got home."

"It's called respecting your privacy," Noah said, wishing he could take back his comment.

His brother quirked an eyebrow up and frowned. "Is that what you call talking to Sierra about it? But whatever. You're right. I'm working on fixing things. A lot of things." It was the most his brother had admitted since he'd been home from Afghanistan. Sierra was having more of an effect than he'd first thought, and he was pleased to find out she'd talked to Bruce. Score another point for the woman he couldn't seem to get out of his head.

They arrived back at the house, preventing Noah from asking more. The sound of laughter coming from the kitchen reached his ears. His mother looked up as they entered.

"Hey, you two. We were just talking about you and how hard you're both working and how much you deserve a break. And I had a great idea," their mother said, her smile one of those oh-no smiles. He'd learned a long time ago it meant she was up to something.

The brothers looked at each other and shrugged, both wary when she turned on the extra sweetness.

"I almost hate to ask," Noah said, glancing at his daughter and Sierra to get a sense if they were involved in her scheme.

"Oh, Daddy. This is something really good, and you simply can't say no," Kaylee was pleading his involvement before he even knew what his mother had cooked up. "We're going on a picnic. You, me, Uncle Bruce, and Sierra."

"I'm just thinking you boys need some fun in your lives." His mother stood there, one hand on a giant basket as though it were a foregone conclusion. At least she'd included Bruce. Otherwise, he'd suspect she was setting him and Sierra up. He took this as another sign his mother approved of her, although, it would seem she hadn't decided for which son.

"Isn't it a bit cold for a picnic?" It was worth a shot, although for a late-October day with the sunshine in full swing, it wasn't as cold as it could be.

"There are these things called jackets, and I've got blankets for you. And I packed hot soup and sandwiches. And if you go on down to the lake, you can walk the trail a bit to get the blood pumping to keep you warm. I'm sure Sierra would love to see it." His mother wasn't taking no for an answer.

"Are you game for this, Sierra? What about your leg?" He hated to ask and put her on the spot, but it had to be done. Bruce hadn't said a word, leaving him to be the one to get everyone to see reason. His mother could be overbearing, and he didn't want to do anything to put Sierra at risk of reinjuring herself.

Sierra's mouth tightened in a straight line, the smile on her face disappearing. He knew she didn't like attention drawn to her injury. "I'm fine. Don't be such a mother hen. You're not my *doctor*." Her emphasis on the last word drove her point home.

"Fine. Far be it for me to put a kink in the plans." Noah shrugged. It was easier to give in than to fight all the female votes that said otherwise. They were outnumbered three to two—a losing battle for sure.

"Yay," Kaylee squealed, jumping off the barstool to come around and hug him.

"Count me out. I've got work to do. I just need a sandwich to hold me to dinner." Bruce shot Noah a look, the hint of a devilish smile on his face.

His brother truly wasn't interested in Sierra that way, but where did that leave Noah? Especially with his brother joining matchmaking forces with their mother.

Chapter Ten

♥

Sierra had only agreed because Bruce was included on the short guest list. Being alone with Noah and his daughter would open up far too much room for more get-to-know-you time, undoubtedly leading to more I-like-you feelings. She already thought about him far too often. And respected him. He'd done things to earn her respect, but not the way Sierra usually responded to.

It was the way he cared for his daughter. His family. His commitment to his job and his promises. And how he went out of his way to watch over her and didn't make it obvious. These weren't things like passing PT tests with the highest score, or running the fastest mile, or even picking the right path in a time of war—or in her case, not picking it.

There was no way out of the arrangement. Laura had already packed the picnic basket; positive no one would say no to her plan. Not to mention, Sierra didn't want to disappoint Kaylee. Everyone needed fresh air now and then, even if it was brisk air. The kind that made one feel alive.

The only real issue was the sly smile on Laura's face. Sierra wouldn't be surprised if things didn't work out exactly as the woman intended. She suspected her efforts were based on matchmaking and not any real sense of outdoor adventure. Sierra was flattered, to say the least.

And by the look of it, it didn't seem to matter which of her sons ended up on the receiving end of her matchmaking, as long as one of them did. It would seem Laura had gotten her answer when Bruce bowed out altogether. But Laura would be disappointed because marriage wasn't in Sierra's cards—not now or in the future. That would require her to let someone else control her life the same way her father controlled her mother's.

No way.

Sierra had caught the look between the two brothers and knew Noah wasn't thrilled either.

Tank had ducked out of this situation in a way he hadn't been able to in the military. That was more than enough reason for her friend to say no. He could do precisely what he wanted.

They loaded up Noah's truck and set off for the nearby White Mountain day-use area. Kaylee sat between them, happily chatting away, oblivious to the awkward silence from the adults.

Noah pulled into the parking lot, where there were surprisingly a few other cars parked. Somehow, hiking trails in the cold had never crossed her mind. Her leg would pay for this tomorrow, but there was no way she was about to admit to anyone she couldn't do it. Her brain had been trained to always meet the challenge, never back down.

"Let's take this trail," Noah said, pointing to the right at the sign junction.

The easy trail. Sierra shot him a disgusted look. "We don't have to take an easy trail because of me, you know."

"It never crossed my mind—I'm doing it for Kaylee." He dared to wink, leaving her suspicious, but how could she argue the obvious. It was for them both, but his comment was a simple reminder to Sierra it wasn't all about her.

Next time, she'd hold her tongue. The easy trail would, without a doubt, save her hide come tomorrow, so no matter what the reason for taking it, she should be grateful—not childish.

"Sorry. That sounds great," Sierra said, hoping he believed her apology. She wasn't prone to giving out platitudes and meant every word.

"Let's go," Kaylee exclaimed, pulling her by the hand. "Daddy can carry the basket, and you and I can be the scouts, watching for wild animals to protect our food."

"You mean to protect your daddy, right?" Sierra teased.

"That too." Kaylee grinned, letting go of Sierra's hand to run ahead. Slow wasn't her speed.

"She's always high energy, but she won't go out of sight. Kaylee knows the rules," Noah quickly reassured her.

"What a great kid, and she adores you."

"Coming in second to the food wasn't flattering, but I'll take it. Kaylee's been a joy beyond belief, especially since the divorce. Before then, I worked way too many hours and didn't spend nearly the time I should have with her, so in a way, the divorce woke me up to what was important in my life." His charming smile disarmed her, and she found herself relaxing, giving in to the moment.

"I think you're doing a wonderful job. It's easy to get caught up in work. It's not that simple to relate to being a child again. Or at least, I imagine it's not. That's why I'm sure I'd make a terrible mom. I have no desire to return to my childhood days." It wasn't a topic she ever discussed, much less brought up, so it surprised her when she uttered the words that could open the hurt locked away in her heart.

"It's not so bad. Besides, I've watched you with Kaylee. I don't think you'd be as bad as you think. When you care about someone, it's a lot easier." Noah's honesty surprised her as much as the compliment.

"I'll take your word on it." She laughed, trying to diffuse the conflicting emotions she felt. Did it come easy with Kaylee because she knew she was leaving or was it easy because it Kaylee being Kaylee? Irresistible.

Sierra cared about her parents, but it's not like she could relate to them. Temporary sounded pretty darn good to her when talking about living with them. Heck, even the three weeks she'd been home after her release from the hospital had been too long. She wasn't feeling the same constriction here that she'd felt at home, even with Noah hovering over like a mother hen at times.

"You're not serious, are you? You don't want marriage and kids or anything down that road? Not even in the future?" He gazed at her, his brow drawn tight.

Not all women wanted the fairy tale, but some men never understood that, lumping all women into the same group. "I am serious. My childhood wasn't exactly perfect. Displays of love and fun and laughter were not really a part of my life. I wouldn't know any other way to be. A child deserves more. Like Kaylee has with you." She couldn't believe she was saying these things, things she'd never told anyone else.

"A person's childhood doesn't control their future unless they let it. Children grow up and can choose what's right for them. Make a difference.

You were effective in the military, or you wouldn't have made it to sergeant. Apply the same dedication to marriage and family, and voila, you would rock it." He made it sound easy, but it simply wasn't true. Sure, she'd made sergeant, but it had been far from easy.

"You haven't met my father. The colonel has a way of taking disappointment to a new level, even with an adult child."

"Colonel? Any chance you're talking about Colonel Winters?" Noah asked, his eyes wide with surprise.

Sierra stopped for a moment. "One and the same. I take it you've heard of him?" Five hours away, and she still couldn't outrun her father's reach.

Noah smiled and shook his head. "Heard of him? More like met him." They resumed walking, with Kaylee still on the move ahead, but in sight. "He gave a lecture at the VA hospital once, offering encouragement to the military soldiers. Talk about a man with a mission and a vision."

Were they discussing the same Colonel Winters? That didn't sound like anything she'd known him to do in the past, but the sincerity of Noah's admiration hit her hard.

"Too bad he never saw his daughter as anything other than a simpering female," she retorted, unable to keep the sarcasm at bay.

"I find that hard to believe. The colonel showed compassion for men and women soldiers alike."

"Like I said, he has different expectations for me. I thought we were out here to enjoy nature, not talk about my life." Sierra moved forward, picking up the pace to join Kaylee and end the unwanted conversation.

Unfortunately, so did Noah. "You can't run from the past. You can keep trying, or you can change, which one you choose is up to you. What's up to me, though, is where we stake out a picnic spot. I know the perfect place. Follow me."

The man was incorrigible, but Sierra laughed and followed his lead—much to her own consternation. Since when did she become a follower? It was true. She didn't mind slowing down and listening to what he had to say or wanted to do for once. She trusted him.

Much the same way she trusted Tank, his brother, and all the other men in her platoon. Except the trust in Noah went beyond that, even if she didn't fully understand why.

Noah led them to a beautiful outcropping of rock that overlooked the valley below. The sun beat down, warming the air, and in return, her. It wasn't as cold as she'd expected. They spread out the blanket his mother had thoughtfully packed, and spent the next hour talking and laughing. Kaylee was quite the character.

Even Noah's common courtesies didn't bother her today. Trivial things like giving her a hand to sit down, or a hand to get up, or when he took the liberty of wiping her mouth with a napkin before awkwardly handing it to her. And then there was the hike to the creek, where he helped her, and then Kaylee, cross the small stone bridge.

The courtesies were extended out of respect for her and his daughter, not because she was lame. The fact she didn't mind, meant there was hope she could still choose to embrace some of her feminine side, just not as a girlfriend.

They passed other happy families who'd had the same idea and were out hiking, hoping to take advantage of the unusually warm day. Sierra couldn't help but wish she'd grown up in a home with so much love instead of her own home's stress. Her mother had never looked as happy as these women.

If Sierra ever did want to play house, Noah was exactly the kind of man she'd want by her side. Strong, attractive, confident. The more time she spent with him, the deeper and more embroiled her feelings were becoming. More reason to be leaving sooner versus later. Between wearing out her welcome and the danger of her heart becoming a doormat, the warning signs were all here.

But the idea of going home didn't appeal. The question was, where did she belong? Because right here, right now, this felt pretty darn good. And judging by Kaylee's resistance to leaving the park, she agreed.

Chapter Eleven

♥

NOAH STILL COULDN'T BELIEVE Sierra was Colonel Winters' daughter. What he hadn't mentioned to her was the fact he'd not only met her father, but he'd also had lunch with him and had been totally impressed with the colonel's commitment to others. Judging by her reaction, he sensed Sierra wouldn't want to hear his opinion of the man.

Letting the subject drop, they walked around a little more, letting Kaylee play.

Thirty minutes later, Kaylee was still pleading to stay. Noah folded, giving in to the inevitable. His daughter didn't turn up her begging level unless it was something she really wanted, and she wanted to spend time with Sierra. Not that Noah couldn't still say no, but he found himself agreeing with Kaylee.

He didn't want the time to end, either. *Like father, like daughter.*

"I've got an idea. Why don't we compromise? How about we leave the park and find a warmer place to hang, like our place. Our new place. We can pick up some dinner and build a fire out on the patio, that is if Sierra would like to come over."

"That's a great idea, Daddy." Kaylee turned to Sierra. "Say you'll come...please."

"What's your new place?" Sierra asked, looking unsure of herself.

"We've got a new house, and it's almost finished. I'm gonna have a great big bedroom and a playroom. And there's a big backyard. Daddy says I can even get a dog." Kaylee's eyes were wide with excitement. He had promised her, and he would stand by the promise, even if it meant more work. His daughter's happiness was paramount to him.

"Wow. I guess by almost finished, it means you're in the process of having it built?" Sierra glanced his way for verification.

"Yup. Daddy's building the whole thing. It's amazing."

Noah grinned and shook his head, not unaffected by his daughter's adoration. "Not the whole thing. I work on it when I can, but I've got builders doing most of the work. There's only so much time in a day, but I promised Kaylee we'd be in our new home by Christmas."

"Well, in that case, I'd love to see the house."

"Then it's all set. We can either stop at Sally's Diner and pick up a dinner basket with some chicken, potatoes, and corn and her famous peach pie, or we can grab a pizza. Whichever you two decide is fine by me," Noah offered, pleased their day together had been extended. He'd forgotten how much fun it could be to do things with other people, and by other people, he meant adults.

Or, in this case, one woman, who had turned this into an outing he'd not soon forget. There was much to be said for making memories with Kaylee, but the special connection between a man and a woman was something he'd forgotten. Until now.

"Yippee," Kaylee squealed. "I pick pizza," she said, grabbing their hands as they made their way to the truck.

"I'm good with that. Pizza's one of my favorites, even if it doesn't like my waistline," Sierra added.

"Why doesn't it like your waistline?" Kaylee asked.

"She means it isn't good for someone watching their weight. Something she doesn't have to worry about." The hint of a smile appeared on Sierra's face, her cheeks blushing prettily.

"Grown-ups can be so confusing," Kaylee said with a shake of her head.

"Pizza it is. I'll text my mom and let her know we won't be home for dinner," Noah said, pulling his phone from his pocket.

"I'm sure your mother will like that. *A lot*." Sierra grinned, stating the obvious.

It was interesting to discover Sierra also knew what his mother was up to and had still agreed to come on the outing. The knowledge went a long way to furthering his own spiral of increasing interest.

After calling in the order, Noah stopped to pick it up, not giving himself time to think of the repercussions. Kaylee was already hooked on Sierra, and Noah wasn't far behind. He was excited to share his home with her, something only his mother and Bruce had been to see up until now. Noah simply didn't share his life with people, and here he was, sharing something very personal, and with a woman, no less.

He couldn't help the twinge of pride that swelled in his chest when they pulled into the driveway. The log home was completely unique and something he'd designed to take advantage of the views. It had been built with doors and windows that opened toward the White Mountains almost seamlessly, as if the mountains were a part of his backyard. The front was rustic, every detail carefully designed to blend with the layout of the land. He'd spent months finishing every detail before they broke ground.

They walked up the front steps, Kaylee leading the way.

"This is incredible. Who was your designer?" Sierra stopped, checking the place out, and expression of awe clearly written on her face.

"Me." Noah shrugged. "I've stored up ideas for ten years, and this—" he gestured toward the log home, "—is a culmination of those dreams." Walking into the house always hit him with a sense of peace. A oneness with the world. But this time, it was more, and he couldn't help but wonder if Sierra was the reason.

"It looks finished. Oh, look at this." She moved across the great room toward the windows as the view captured her attention. "It's like entering a new world. One where you can see forever. It's odd though, I feel like I've seen this place before. It's not possible, but just a feeling."

"I love it here. And you might not be wrong about recognizing the area." He grinned.

"What do you mean? Oh," she exclaimed, her eyes growing wide. "The painting in your room at the ranch. I love it. But you didn't actually paint it, did you?"

"I did." Noah didn't want to make a big deal of it. He was a novice painter, but her reaction meant something to him. When he'd first discovered the spot, he'd known where he wanted to build the house. The painting had been his reminder while the house was being built.

"That's incredible. Each time I gaze at it, I feel like I'm in the picture. I hope you bring it here. I can see why you love this spot. You need two oversized armchairs that make one want to stop and enjoy the beauty. It's the perfect place to sit and watch wildlife. Or read. Or just do nothing. It's like the place speaks calming words as one looks into the vastness."

Sierra totally nailed the way he felt every time he stood in this very spot, absorbing the stillness and beauty of Mother Nature. "I totally agree. I hadn't thought of a chair in this spot, though it's a great idea." He laughed. "But I had thought of the rest of what you said."

"Add a small table, and voila, you have a magical escape to the great outdoors." What she described sounded perfect, especially if Sierra was an occupant in one of those chairs. An image of him bringing her coffee on a chilly morning crossed his mind.

"Let me show you the rest of the place, and then we can sit outside to eat, and I'll get a fire going. We come out here to eat when we have time, but it's been at least a week since I've been here. I want to check on the guys' progress. They are completing a couple of rooms and then cleaning up the place. They've promised it will be ready by the first week in December, which is only a little over a month away." It was also when Sierra had to report back to duty, something he didn't want to focus on.

It had been a long year since the divorce, something made more difficult by moving home to help his mother six months ago. But now, with the house almost finished and his brother home to stay, he was looking forward to moving to the new place. Not that he wasn't grateful he had his family home to go to. He was. It was just time to be on his own again. Not that he wasn't grateful he had his family home to go to. He was. It was just time to be on his own again.

"And then you're moving out of your mom's? What does she think of that? Seems to me she likes having you both there." Sierra moved to check out the kitchen, running her long fingers along the countertop's ceramic tile.

Noah frowned. It was never his intention to upset his mother. "I imagine she does, but seriously, I never saw myself living with my mother for the rest of my life. That's not the way things are done. It was only temporary, and she knew it."

Sierra looked back at him and smiled, dimples deepening at the corners of her mouth. The image made him want to kiss her.

"I'm going out back, Dad," Kaylee called out. She stood at the back door that led outside to the deck.

"Okay, we'll be right there. Don't go off the deck until we're ready to go downstairs." He trusted her and felt sure she'd be safe, but until he got more accustomed to the surroundings, those were his rules. Not that Kaylee hadn't vocally disagreed more than once.

The door closed behind his daughter, and Noah turned to face Sierra. "Sorry about her coercion tactics to spend more time with you." He watched Kaylee dance around out on the deck, a free spirit for sure.

"Don't worry about it. It's flattering." He was rewarded with another of Sierra's special smiles.

"I do worry though because Kaylee would like nothing better than to find me a wife. My plans, on the other hand, don't include another relationship." Adding the last part was self-preservation. He didn't want another relationship, but he wasn't so sure when it came to Sierra.

"What? What about your ex-wife? Doesn't Kaylee want you to get back together with her? I thought that was every child's dream when it comes to divorced parents."

Most kids, but not Kaylee. His daughter had been through a lot, but together, the two of them had ridden out the storm of Blanche's departure and were now in a much better place. His daughter simply thought she could wave her magic wand and find him a wife and her a mother. It didn't take a rocket scientist to realize Kaylee coming out of her shell for Sierra, meant she'd set her sights on her being the one chosen. "Not that I can tell. I think she wants to see her mom more, but Blanche has her own ideas of what motherhood means, and it doesn't include a lot of time with a kid."

"That's a shame. She's a lovely young girl." Sierra turned to watch Kaylee doing handstands on the deck.

"Tell me about it." Noah grinned, more than willing to hear praise of the little girl who held the only key to his heart.

"You two are a wonderful team. She idolizes you."

"And you." He nodded, casting a glance in Sierra's

direction, curious how she'd react. It's not as if she could be blind to the fact, but sometimes people didn't see what was right in front of their faces.

"It would seem that way. I'm sorry if it makes things harder for you. I don't want to hurt her when I leave, but it can't be helped." Sierra crossed her arms in front of her chest as if putting a wall between them.

Nothing he didn't already know, but it was nice to hear her say it. "I've tried to explain it to her, but she insists you two will be best friends forever." Noah understood his daughter's position all too well.

She nodded. "So what happened with Blanche? If you don't mind my asking, that is."

"We used to have fun together, and mistakenly thought it was love. We got married before we really talked about the future. The two of us were on completely different planes, and when she accidentally got pregnant, she blamed me. She tried for a few years to deal with the change in plans, but in the end, it simply wasn't the life she wanted, and she left." It was almost a year later, and his self-reproach for his youthful stupidity hadn't wavered in the least.

Sierra reached out to touch his arm. "I'm sorry," she said, her voice filled with genuine emotion.

Noah didn't move. Couldn't move. He was unwilling to break the connection between them. "Don't be. It's not your fault, and I wouldn't change a thing. Having my daughter in my life is worth every- thing I've been through." Best stupid thing he'd ever done.

"What a wonderful attitude." She dropped her gaze to where her hand still held his arm, her cheeks bright pink. An awkward awareness filled the air, and Sierra stepped back.

"Only attitude to have. I figure the two of us are doing fairly good as a team, and as soon as the house is finished, things will be perfect." At least for him. Kaylee would still want a mother figure to have a starring role in her life, but Noah was content with things just as they were. Wasn't he? Sierra was the first person he'd met since his divorce that made him question his choice of a solitary life.

He led Sierra out the back door and down the stairs toward the picnic table and fire ring.

Kaylee followed, taking charge by carrying the pizza. She set the box in the middle of the table and spread the napkins out for each person, designating the seating spaces. "You both sit on that side." She pointed to the opposite side of the table, just to be sure he understood. "I'm over here." She smiled, brooking no opposition to her orders as she sat down at her place.

It put him and Sierra sitting next to each other. Close. The apple clearly didn't fall from the grandmother tree. Both were trying to do a bit of matchmaking.

Sierra smelled of sweet lemony citrus, a scent he'd come to recognize whenever he was around her. It was like freshness in a bottle.

"I haven't been to a pizza party in ages. What a great idea," Sierra said.

Kaylee beamed. They ate and talked, his daughter taking the lead and talking about everything from the food she liked and disliked, to activities, clothes, colors, and favorite dream vacations. Noah knew it for what it was. Kaylee was on a fact-finding mission on his behalf. It wasn't long before they were finished eating, and the endless supply of energy, in the form of a little girl, announced they needed to play tag.

"Except I can't run as fast as you can," Sierra said.

Noah winced, realizing too late he should have immediately nixed the idea.

"You mean cause of your hurt leg?" Kaylee looked up at Sierra, a serious expression etched on her face.

"No, cause you're the fastest girl in your class at school." Sierra shot a wink and a grin in Noah's direction.

"Yup. I am. I can't wait till you see me race at the jubilee."

"I'm looking forward to it." Sierra nodded and stood, ready to accept the challenge.

Noah admired her attitude, one which was quite different from when she'd first arrived at the Jackson ranch. He could only hope she continued down the same road toward recovery. They played for half an hour before he could tell Sierra had had enough, doing more hobbling than walking. Kaylee ran toward the side of the house, and Noah followed. "Tag, you're it," he said laughingly as he lunged for his daughter.

"Oh, no, not again." She grimaced.

"Not this time, so you're off the hook. We need to pack up and head home. You've got school in the morning." Noah used his dad's-in-charge voice, hoping to end any chance of a scene. "Can you run the pizza box and napkins to the trash can in the house?" he asked.

"*Bah humbug*." To his daughter's credit, she gave in and headed for the stairs, quickly disappearing into the house, and leaving him alone with Sierra to follow.

Sierra grabbed for a bottle of water on the table at the same time he did, their fingers touching. During the game, there'd been a couple of moments where they'd bumped into one another. With Kaylee watching, he'd withdrawn instantly, quelling any foreign thoughts about what it would be like to kiss her.

This close, his brain drifted back to the idea. Only this time, his daughter wasn't here to offer him protection from himself. *To kiss or not to kiss.*

Giving in to the urge, Noah reached for her hand. He intertwined his fingers with hers, gently keeping her close and increasing the awareness between them and signaling his intentions. He leaned forward and dropped a kiss on her lips, surprising himself when it turned into more than a peck.

Kissing was kissing. However, more surprising, was that Sierra didn't resist his attempts to deepen the lip-lock they shared. Having crossed the line, what was a little more? He might not have the chance again.

"Daddy, you..." his daughter called from the upper deck.

Noah pulled away and shot her a glance. It was evident from her expression that Kaylee had seen them.

"Were you two kissing?" Kaylee asked, a broad smile on her face.

"I had something in my eye..." Sierra started to say.

His daughter knew better, and Noah always taught her honesty was best. "*Ummm*, yes. We were, but—"

"Does that mean you're getting married?" Kaylee asked, her eyes wide with delight.

"No, honey. We're just friends, and it was purely by accident." Although what that meant, he wasn't sure. There was nothing unexpected about it, nor did he believe in accidental kisses. You either wanted to, or you didn't. And he did.

Had. Past tense.

Once had to be enough. Sierra had made it clear she wasn't interested in relationships, marriage, or anything in between. Only a fool would give in to the urge a second time. Especially given it wasn't as if he wanted to go down the happily-ever-after road again.

Except, in his case...it could be his first trip down that road. Something worth considering. But later. Right now, he needed to focus on convincing Kaylee it didn't mean a thing. Otherwise, by bedtime, his whole family would know about the kiss.

Chapter Twelve

❤

SIERRA LED SUGAR TO the creek for a drink of water. It had been another tiring day at Whispering Pines, and the solo ride was supposed to help clear the thoughts swirling in her head ever since Noah's kiss. She'd spent three whole days trying to eradicate them, but the harder she tried, the more they consumed her. The problem was she'd liked it. The connection. But it wasn't part of her plan to develop feelings for someone. *What if it clouded her judgment?*

And what of Noah? She hadn't seen much of him lately. Coincidence or planned?

Her foot caught on something, causing her to stumble and grab her calf as excruciating pain ripped down her leg. Bent over, she grimaced, fighting back the urge to cry out. It had been a careless move, but it was a strong, painful reminder she was far from healed and still useless. Who was she kidding? She didn't belong here. She couldn't let people rely on her when she wasn't at her best.

Rhaegar was another failure in a long line of them. There was still no word on his location, and she was beginning to think some of the stories she'd heard were true. Reports that handlers weren't always given the first choice or even considered when it came to adopting discharged canine soldiers. She'd contacted Mission K-9 and the American Humane organizations, but so far, they hadn't turned up anything on his whereabouts either.

Everywhere she turned, she was reminded of her shortcomings. She'd gone from being on top of her game to the bottom of the mud pit. It would be easier to leave and face her parents' condemnation than that of the Jackson family and her new friends at Whispering Pines.

Sierra had enjoyed the past week working with the kids in the *GiddyUp* program, and some of the other riding groups—but it wasn't enough. Chad and his wife tried to make her feel welcome and wanted, but all she did was lead the trail rides. Not to mention that on the *GiddyUp* rides, an adult always brought up the rear.

Did they normally have a rider at the back, or was it because of her injury and inability to help in a situation if needed? Maybe this was nothing more than a pity party.

Limping toward the nearest big log, she hoisted herself up, using Sugar as leverage, and managed to slide back into the saddle. At least no one would have to come looking for her when she didn't return. Talk about mortifying. She'd take the pain over humiliation and was glad no one had witnessed her most recent stupidity.

Arriving back at the barn, her luck wasn't as good.

"Have a nice ride?" Chad called out as he met her at the hitching post.

"Absolutely," she lied, grimacing through the pain as she landed on her left leg gingerly, but not gingerly enough to quell the ache firing down her nerves.

With one raised eyebrow and a tight set to his lips, Chad nodded. "Great. I'll brush down Sugar if you want to head out." He knew. And she knew he knew.

Offering to help was his way to baby her, and she wanted to refuse. It was the same look of pity she saw on people's faces when they noticed her uneven gait. More so when she used her cane.

But with each step she took, there could only be one answer if she intended to save face. "That would be great," she said, her voice holding a false lilt. "Kaylee wanted me to help her with a project tonight." It was true, but it was *after* dinner and not before.

"See you tomorrow?" he asked, his gaze never leaving her face.

"Of course." *Maybe, maybe not.* Sierra simply wasn't sure this was in the best interests of anyone involved. The kids. The Andrews. Or her.

She drove back to the Jackson ranch, hoping Tank was around. He'd shoot straight with her. They'd grown closer lately, their mutual talks both private and encouraging as they helped each other. Today, Sierra needed to talk about sticking around or throwing in the towel. Her vote was for the towel.

Dinner was a drawn-out affair between Kaylee's constant conversation, Tank's assessing looks, and Noah's determination to push for information about her day. He'd seen her limp was more pronounced, but she'd avoided being alone with him to stave off his medical questions.

Laura, on the other hand, watched everything, speaking little. Which, in hindsight, wasn't a good thing considering how close she'd become lately with the older woman. Her earlier comments about her son's availability left no doubt in Sierra's mind about what the woman was up to. And her silence now, if Sierra had a guess, was her trying to figure out which way the wind blew. She didn't understand the wind would blow Sierra right out their lives and back to the base. It was the only place she'd known as home since high school.

The Army was a constant in her life, even if she had moved bases a few times. She'd been at her last post for four years, and if she re-upped, it was guaranteed to come with another move. It was her life and something she'd always enjoyed, up until now. Now, she wasn't sure about anything.

"Tank, can I give you a hand in the barn?" Code for she wanted to talk.

"Sure thing. I'm headed out now." He pushed back from the table and stood.

Noah watched them, his eyes darkening a bit, but other than that, he gave no reaction.

"You two run along. I'll get the table. Noah can help me." Laura laughed, gathering up a couple of plates.

"Thanks. I promise it'll be my turn tomorrow," Sierra said, provided she stuck around, of course.

"Will you be back in time to tuck me in?" Kaylee asked with a frown.

"Definitely. I promise." She smiled and stopped to drop a kiss on the girl's head. Her childish adoration was a bit overwhelming but not unwanted. Sierra hadn't done anything to earn the girl's respect, and yet she'd given it willingly. The innocence of a child yet to learn the ways of the world. Colonel Winters's world anyway.

Tank let her exit through the back door first. For once, Sierra didn't analyze why. She had more important things on her mind.

"So, what's up? I know you didn't just volunteer to help me to get out of doing dishes." He chuckled, falling in step next to her.

"True. Something happened today and I want your honest opinion. And you can't tell a soul." She grabbed his arm, forcing him to look at her.

Tank quirked an eyebrow up, the frown on his face a tell-tale sign of worry mixed with doubt. "Depends on what it is."

"Tank...come on. Promise me," she urged.

He shrugged, albeit a bit reluctantly. "Fine. I promise."

"I tripped—over a log. It's why I'm limping more. The pain is killing me." Sierra was loathed to admit the truth, but she couldn't get her friend's honest opinion if she didn't tell him. Not to mention, they were trying to help each other through some tough stuff, and this was all part of hers.

He paused. "What happened? That's not like you to misstep."

"I was thinking about things and missed it. The why isn't as important as the what's next." Especially since she'd been thinking about Noah. No way did she want Tank to have that kind of information. She wasn't sure if he'd put it to appropriate use.

He continued toward the barn, taking her words at face value. "What's the problem then?" he asked.

"I don't think I should stay here any longer. I can't do any real work in the barn. I'm terrified of doing something wrong with the *GiddyUp* kids. I'm worried about Kaylee's growing attachment to me." She said it all in a rush, relieved to let it all out.

Tank grabbed her arm and stopped walking, turning her to face him. "Wow. That's putting a lot of pressure on yourself. And leaving is a cop-out. Totally unlike you. I need to know more about what's behind this. And for the record, I don't think you should leave yet. I don't want you to leave yet." He said the last in a hushed tone, as if he wasn't sure how she'd receive it.

Did Tank like her? One more reason to leave. Tank wasn't the one she was interested in, and it wouldn't do any good to serve him a plate of rejection on top of everything else he was dealing with. She wanted friendship, nothing more.

"Tank—"

"Hear me out. I think the place has been good for you emotionally, even if you've had a few setbacks with your leg. Give it time. More important is the mental healing I see in you, and that I see in me."

She let out the breath she'd been holding. He wasn't talking about more than friendship and wanted her to stay because it was good for them both.

"But what if something happens? I don't want to be responsible for anything that goes wrong. Not again," she squeaked out the last two words under her breath.

"Sierra, let it go." Tank stepped closer and pulled her into a hug. Strong and secure and...brotherly, she hoped.

She pulled back. "Earlier, you said you wanted me to stay. As a friend—right?" she asked, needing to make sure she wasn't creating more problems than she could manage. One Jackson brother was enough.

"Of course. What...oh. No worries." He chuckled. "I'm still with the girl in Boston. One of these days, I'll bring her home. Maybe for Thanksgiving. I'd like you to meet her."

Sierra was filled with relief. Far too often, friendships were destroyed when someone developed romantic feelings that weren't reciprocated. "Sounds nice. I'm not sure I'll be here that long. I just don't know. But thanks for making me feel wanted."

"I'm not asking you to stay just for me." Tank's voice had dropped a notch as if imparting secret information.

She couldn't stop from taking the bait. "What do you mean?"

"Noah." Tank dropped the one-word bomb as expertly as he had on some of the missions they'd been on together.

"What about Noah?" She stopped, determined to get him to explain.

"I think he likes you. Blanche was all wrong for him, but I think you'd be good for him. That you'd be good together. Not that my brother would listen to me." Tank dropped the second bomb as efficiently as the first. It was the last thing Sierra had expected to hear. Talk about being unprepared.

Ambushed is more like it.

"Don't you dare say a word to encourage him, Tank Jackson. I'm not on the market." It was better to put an end to his wayward thoughts quickly, and not let Tank start filling her head with nonsense and dreams. It was a good thing she hadn't told him the truth about the kiss or her mixed-up feelings. She knew he would've gone straight to Noah with the information.

"But you could be. And you two *did* meet in the market." He laughed, jogging a short way away from her as she tried to punch his arm in protest.

"You heard me, Tank. Not a word. And one day, when this leg is better, I'll make you pay if you do say anything." Her inability to chase him and keep up, drove home her current shortcomings, which only added to her frustrations.

"I wouldn't be foolish enough to tell you if I did, Sergeant Winters." Tank saluted and walked off, the grin on his face one she couldn't wipe away. Not just yet anyway.

Sierra headed back to the house, thinking over what Tank had told her and trying to decide. Laura, Tank, and Kaylee had all made it clear she was wanted here and welcome to stay. Something she hadn't felt in a long time. But what about Noah?

He'd kissed her, and since then, he'd done the vanishing act every chance he got.

I think he likes you. Tank's words echoed in her ear. Except Noah had made it clear on multiple occasions that his life had to remain focused on Kaylee, and he wasn't looking to repeat the mistake of marriage. Perhaps the kiss had been a mistake, and he knew it.

So where did that leave Sierra? What would she do if Noah did have room in his heart? Was Laura right? Was there more to life for Sierra than just the military? Noah was the first man to make her consider such a thing but putting her heart on the line seemed too great a risk.

Sierra's phone rang, her mother's ringtone made her cringe. Her mother had been pressing her to come home for Thanksgiving, but Sierra kept putting off the decision. At least until she had been putting it off, until today when she'd tripped over the log, a painful reminder of everything she couldn't and shouldn't do.

"Hey, Mom. What's up?" She forced gaiety she wasn't feeling into her voice.

"Checking in on you. You know I worry about you. Are you doing your exercises? I don't know why you haven't come home. I liked taking care of you." Her mother had a habit of rambling on, only stopping to take a breath now and then and to let someone answer. Talk about high energy.

"I know, but I needed a change of scenery. The leg is doing better," Sierra fibbed. If her mother knew the truth, she'd call out the big gun in the shape of the colonel and try to force her to come home.

"Good to know, dearie. I hesitate to mention this because I know how independent you are. But your father wanted me to pass along some information."

Something coming in backhandedly from the colonel didn't bode well. "What is it, Mother?"

"Your father found a job for you working at Schuster's, a local insurance agency here in Boston. He wants you to come home and check it out. He promised the guy you'd talk to him the day after Thanksgiving. You really should consider getting a discharge considering your new situation. Having you back home is all your father talks about." At times like these, her mother's ramblings left her on edge, the information overload revealing far more than the facts.

Sierra shook her head, fighting back the tears. This was precisely why she didn't want to go home. Her dad tried to control her life. He'd never wanted her in the military, and even after ten years, he hadn't changed his mind. Sierra was tired of his negativity.

I think he likes you. Tank's words echoed in her head again. Was there something worth sticking around for with Noah and the rest of the Jackson family as a bonus? A real family. "I'm sorry, Mother. I won't be home for Thanksgiving. I promised Mrs. Jackson I'd stay and help with her granddaughter. I'll stop in before I report back to base, I promise."

"But, Sierra, it's Thanksgiving. You should be with your family. And what do I tell your father about the job offer?"

"Tell the colonel to go to the interview himself since he made the appointment. I have a job. Two, in fact. Got to run, Mother. Good night." Her mother had always fallen in step with the colonel. She was utterly in love and clueless in Sierra's opinion.

She disconnected the call before her mother had a chance to counter her arguments. The pain in her leg demanded she get off her feet, and a warm bed on a chilly night sounded perfect. It would give her more time to think about the future. The past had been easy, with no worry for anyone other than herself. She'd been able to commit wholeheartedly to her military career.

But it was the future she was worried about because now Noah and Kaylee were in the picture. Based on the declaration she'd made to her mother; her decision was made.

Sierra was staying.

Something that might make denying her developing feelings for Noah difficult.

Chapter Thirteen

♥

DRIVING HOME FROM WORK, Noah couldn't help the extra rush of pleasure knowing he'd soon be seeing Kaylee and Sierra. After the kiss, things had changed between them. There was a new wariness of sorts. But no matter what he thought he wanted, he kept coming back around to the only honest answer. After fighting the attraction for days, he wanted to kiss her again. He wanted to talk to her about sticking around or coming back when she was on leave in the future.

Seal the deal. Then Noah would know how she felt about him and if there was even a remote possibility of a *them*. Tonight, he intended to make his feelings known. Cowardice wasn't a part of his genetic makeup.

He glanced around as he pulled up close to the house and parked. No one was on the porch, and he wondered if dinner was being served early tonight. If it was, whatever he wanted to say to Sierra would have to wait until later. Noah pushed open the door and called out, "Mom? Kaylee? Anyone in here?"

"In the kitchen, Noah," his mother called out from, her voice chipper as always. After they'd returned from the picnic, it was as if his mother carried around a secret—only Noah knew exactly what she knew. She would have been the first one Kaylee told that night, but his mother hadn't said a word to him, much to her credit.

On the other hand, he was sure Bruce had been kept out of the loop. His mother was keeping all her options open by the look of things. The idea of Bruce and Sierra together soured him a bit and rocked his resolution to speak to her. He was not wholly sure where things stood. It wasn't like Noah had ever experienced a good, close relationship with a woman.

And then there was still the mystery woman in his brother's life.

"It was a slow day, and I cut out early," he said, dropping a kiss on her weathered cheek.

"That's great. I'll add a place for you at the table. You're just in time for some macaroni and cheese. You boys always loved it, and Kaylee takes after you."

"That's because you make it better than they do over at O'Malley's, and that's saying a lot." He grinned.

"Flattery will get you everywhere. Maybe an extra plateful tonight? Do me a favor and call everyone in? They're out back somewhere."

"Sounds good to me, and I'm on it." Noah headed out the back door and glanced around. He didn't see anyone at first until a flash of color near the barn caught his eye. The sight of Bruce and Sierra locked in an embrace stopped him in his tracks. Noah's stomach clenched with jealousy, a completely un- nat- ural response he didn't much care for.

The two separated, and Noah let out the breath he'd been holding. *Friends*. Sierra said so. Bruce said so. And he trusted them. Shoving any nega- tive thoughts aside, he continued toward the barn.

Bruce had already gone back inside before he got there.

"Evening, Sierra," he said as he drew near.

She jumped just enough for him to realize he'd taken her by surprise. Guilt? No. He wouldn't go down that road. She had a lot going on, but Bruce wasn't on her agenda. She'd kissed Noah like she cared, and nothing about Sierra came across as fake.

"You startled me. You're home early," she said, glancing down at her watch. "Kaylee will be excited. She made a Thanksgiving decoration in school and she's eager to show you."

"I can't wait." He wished there was time to talk to her now, seeing as they were alone. Unfortunately, there wasn't that much time. "And speaking of not waiting, Mom's got dinner ready, and I was sent to round you all up. I saw Bruce head back into the barn, but where's Kaylee?" His voice had an edge he didn't like, but it couldn't be helped. Seeing the two of them hugging irritated him beyond words. And he didn't like that he didn't like it.

Sierra cocked her head to one side as if analyzing what he'd said, her brow furrowing ever so slightly.

"Bruce was helping me with something. He just went back in the barn, and Kaylee's in there playing with the calves."

Noah wasn't going to ask her to clarify. That's what trust was all about. "Okay." He nodded.

They started toward the barn doors. "Bruce gave me some words of encouragement. I heard from my mother again today, and it wasn't pretty. My father's adamant I come home for Thanksgiving, and you know my feelings on the subject." Her father was always a sore spot.

"It's your life. Do what you want to do. You're old enough not to have to make decisions to please your parents, colonel or no colonel."

"You sound just like Tank." She laughed.

Noah grinned. "It's the Jackson mentality of No Worries—Be Happy."

"I'll go call Kaylee. Bruce should be around back. See if you can convince him to take a break from working on the water trough he's repairing."

"Dinner's mac and cheese. It'll be a race to see who gets there first and who gets the most." He laughed when her eyes shot wide open in surprise. "Don't worry, Mom knows us and makes a ton."

Sierra shook her head and laughed as she walked away, disappearing behind the barn door.

Noah found his brother just where Sierra told him he'd be. "Mom's got dinner ready."

Bruce paused, glancing up momentarily before returning to work on the trough. "You're home early. Just a few more minutes, I'll be right up." He hammered in a new nail.

"Okay, more for me till you get there," Noah said, handing him the next nail.

"Thanks. Why more for you? What's for dinner?" His brother paused with a questioning expression on his face.

"Mac and cheese night."

Bruce tossed his hammer and work belt on the bench nearby, shooting Noah a grin as he tipped back his hat. "Let's see if you can beat me to the table. Race you, old man."

"I'm waiting for Kaylee and Sierra. You go ahead."

"Wow. You really do have it bad for Sierra. Kaylee said as much, but I'm impressed." So, his daughter *had* been telling tales out of school. Okay, so not tales. The truth. That was worth giving up an extra share of mac and cheese any day.

The barn door opened, and Sierra rushed out and toward them.

"Tank, have you seen Kaylee? She was playing with the calves, but now she's not even in the barn," Sierra said the words in a rush, fear evident in her voice.

But nowhere near the heart-stopping fear Noah felt. He knew she wasn't in the house or with Bruce. And if she wasn't in the barn... He didn't want to think of the impending night or the dangers on a ranch. They had to find her.

"Let's circle around the barn and check the shed. Bruce, you can check inside the barn again. You know the nooks and crannies to play hide and seek in. She's probably just having a little fun with us." At least, that's what Noah hoped, saying a silent prayer.

Ever since he started filling the single-parent role, his life had been a roller coaster of emotion. Worry. Fear. Love. Laughter. Right now, he wanted to get rid of the concern lodged in his gut.

"Sure thing," Bruce said, heading for the barn in double time.

"Sierra, you go around that way, and I'll meet you in back at the shed," Noah ordered, pointing to the right of the barn.

"Okay. I'm sorry, Noah. I don't know what happened. I swear she was in the barn, and then I got a call from my mom..." The minute Sierra realized what she was saying, tears glistened in her eyes, threatening to fall. "I knew it—it's my fault. I got distracted."

"So far, nothing's happened. Let's search, then we'll talk about it. Okay?" Fear had Noah silently agreeing with her assessment. She was at fault. With a child, you could never lose focus. Kaylee would be all right. She had to be. Between lecturing his daughter on disappearing, and dealing with Sierra's lack of responsibility, there would be many discussions ahead. For now, his focus had to remain on finding Kaylee.

"Okay." She nodded. They each went a separate route, Noah's heart racing double time when he didn't find his daughter and both Sierra and Bruce turned up empty-handed.

"What do you want to do now? It's going to get dark soon." His brother was aware of the dangers.

"We search until we find her. Bruce, head up to the house and check for Kaylee there, just to be sure she didn't slip by me. And let Mom know what's going on. Tell her to stay put and call Captain Taylor to give the police the heads-up. If we don't find her in the next half hour, I want the captain to call in the Hallbrook Rescue Squad to lend a hand in the search. If Kaylee shows up at the house, have Mom call us. If you'll get the truck and follow the river, Sierra and I will follow the tree line. Call me if you spot her or any sign she's been there. This isn't like her. At all." Which is why the fear had blown up inside him to suffocating proportions.

"Will do, but Noah, remember, she knows the area, and she's smart. We'll find Kaylee. She likes to explore." His brother was trying to offer him a reason to stay calm, but it wouldn't work. He wouldn't be calm until they found his daughter.

Noah prayed it was all a mistake, and she was back at the house playing with her dolls. "I realize the truth of what you're saying, but all her explorations have involved an adult. All but this one, apparently."

"Don't start jumping to conclusions. Let's work together, and we'll find her. I'm good at this reconnaissance stuff, and you've got another expert with you. Just minus her dog." His brother clapped him on the back as he glanced apologetically at Sierra.

"I'm trying. I promise." It was harder than they could imagine. Kaylee wasn't their child.

"Tank's right. We'll find her, Noah," Sierra said with more worry than reassurance in her voice.

"We better," he snapped.

Sierra pulled back, shocked at his tone. No more so than he was, but it was too late to take it back. Besides, if anything happened to his daughter, he wouldn't want to take it back. Sierra was responsible. Maybe she'd been right all along, and she wasn't fit to be a parent.

Noah grabbed a flashlight off the barn wall and headed for the woods, Sierra close on his heels. She hadn't answered his comment, but she didn't have to judging by the expression on her face. He'd hurt her, and she was blaming herself. A powerful combination that would fell the best of soldiers.

If it was about anyone other than his daughter, he might have given Sierra a pass. But she was the one responsible for keeping an eye on Kaylee, and she'd gotten caught up in the call with her mother and then Bruce.

Kaylee has a mind of her own sometimes, and you're not perfect, either. The voice in his head rang out loud and clear. A message from God, perhaps? But one he chose to ignore.

Chapter Fourteen

♥

SIERRA TRIED TO FOCUS on searching for Kaylee, but Noah's anger echoed her own, and the combination made it difficult stop the torrent of images flashing in her brain. The past coming to life. Another time when she was running through the woods. The explosion. And then everything turned black. Sierra stumbled. Shoving aside the memories, she regrouped, Noah none the wiser to her misstep.

His focus remained pinned to the woods searching for his daughter, his booming voice calling out to her.

She'd failed a critical task. *Again.* Her father was right—maybe it was time to get out of the military. Or if she stayed, to take a desk job where mistakes wouldn't be so shattering. Tears filled her eyes. She brushed them away as she continued to call out

Kaylee's name, over and over. Darkness was closing in on them, and Sierra's fear suffocated her.

A spot of bright pink appeared from the woods. Kaylee coming toward them. *Thank you, Lord.*

Noah glanced her way. "Call Bruce and my mom and let them know we found her," he shouted as he took off running. He lifted Kaylee into his arms and held her tight as he swung her around.

Sierra called Tank, who said he'd let their mother know. Relief was evident in his voice, echoing her own sentiments. As she drew closer, Kaylee seemed dejected, but physically, she looked fine.

"What were you thinking, Kaylee?" Noah asked, the fear in his voice easing as he held her and kept checking her over to reassure himself that she was okay.

"I saw a dog, Daddy, and I tried to pet him. He ran away, so I went to find him. He looked lost and alone and like he needed a friend," Kaylee said, sounding quite tired.

"But, Kaylee, you can't run off without a grown-up. We've been worried sick about you." He nuzzled his face into her neck, and Sierra could tell he was fighting for control. Everything he held most dear in his life was in his arms and safe.

"I'm okay, Daddy. I'm a big girl." Kaylee did act older than her age sometimes, but Sierra was positive it wasn't the approach to take if she wanted to calm her father down. It was clear he wanted his little girl to always be his little girl, and right now, she couldn't blame Noah for being upset. Kaylee was only seven.

"Not that big, pumpkin."

She couldn't imagine the emotional rollercoaster he'd been on since discovering Kaylee missing. It was also a painful reminder that the soldier who'd died because of her decision that fateful day, also had parents whose hearts had been broken beyond repair. How did families deal with the loss?

God. Through God, people could find strength and hope to carry them through tough times. Sierra could only hope Private Brady's family had found the answers they needed to deal with their loss. Not for the first time, Sierra wondered if she should pay them a visit to honor his memory. Witnessing Noah and Kaylee's emotions as an outsider made her realize that sometimes, the best a person could do was be there to offer support.

Kaylee's eyes filled with tears. "But, Daddy, you always taught me to kind and helpful, and that's what I was doing."

"What do you mean?" he asked, his brow furrowed tight.

"The dog. It was all black, just like the doggy Miss Sierra had and can't find. I wanted to give the dog to her to make her feel better so she wouldn't cry no more," Kaylee said, her voice taking on a slightly defensive whine. But it was the words that broke Sierra's heart.

Kaylee had put herself at risk for her.

She stepped forward to hug Kaylee. "Thank you, sweetheart. What a thoughtful idea, but I'll find my dog, I promise. I'm not giving up until I do. It's okay to cry sometimes when you miss someone." It was something Sierra hadn't allowed herself the luxury of until recently. Crying was generally for the weak, or so she used to believe. Life had a way of changing her view. "You really shouldn't have run off, but your generosity is overwhelming."

Noah was surprisingly quiet as Sierra spoke, letting her take the lead response.

"I just wanted you to feel better." Kaylee's mouth formed a pout in frustration. Clearly, she didn't understand why everyone was so concerned.

"I agree with Sierra. You have a big heart, and the idea was sweet, but you can't break the rules to do those kind-hearted things. One offsets the other. I don't want anything to happen to my precious baby girl."

"I'm sorry, Daddy." Kaylee's tears started to fall in earnest.

Tank pulled up in the truck and jumped out. "Everything okay?"

"She's fine. Just out for a walk with a dog she doesn't own." Noah shook his head and shot her a look before turning back to his brother. "I'll explain later. Can you take her back to the house and get her some dinner?" Noah asked, already carrying Kaylee to the truck under the assumption anything he asked would be done. "Sierra and I will be right behind you. We need to talk." The tone of Noah's voice didn't bode well.

"You got it. Glad you're okay, kiddo," Tank said, ruffling his niece's hair.

"It was just a walk, Uncle Bruce. Of course, I'm okay." Kaylee was brushing away her tears and back to being the brave little girl who'd stood her ground moments ago.

Another look passed between the two men. This time it was one Sierra fully understood. They were lucky Kaylee was okay. Tank drove away, kicking up the dust a bit.

Alone with Noah, Sierra worried what he'd have to say now that the danger had passed. He'd let Kaylee off the hook, but Sierra wasn't holding out any such hope. And she deserved his wrath. When he didn't speak, she took the bull by the horns, wanting to get it over. "I'm sorry. I know it's my fault—"

"Your darn right it is. You were in charge of watching her. Instead, you were fraternizing with my brother long enough to let her out of your sight to wander off. Something she wouldn't have done if it weren't for you and your missing dog. She's an impressionable child and sees your pain in black and white. It's too much for her to understand."

Sierra recoiled from the attack. She'd expected his wrath, but his disdain and accusation, not so much. Her respect for Noah dropped a notch. Unrealistic expectations were always a person's downfall. "You're right. I should have been watching her better. I can accept that, and I thank God she's okay. But as to the other stuff... You can't expect me to not talk about the one thing I value most in life with people I consider friends. That's way beyond a reasonable expectation."

"Like I said...she's impressionable. Sometimes you have to think of the impact of involving others. Kaylee's safety is my number-one concern." He wasn't backing down.

She understood he was upset, and this was an irrational release of emotion. Still, it didn't take away the bitter sting of his words. It also made her decision a whole lot easier. Soon, everyone would get what they wanted. Except her, of course. "Well, she's safe. You've done your job. I'm only sticking around until the jubilee for Kaylee in order to keep my promise. I'll leave right after it, and you won't have to worry about my bad influence anymore. I'm sure we can figure out a way to avoid each other until then."

"That might be best." Any thought that Noah might backtrack disappeared. Along with it went any chance for the two of them. More proof she wasn't suited to relationships or family.

The two walked the rest of the way to the house in silence. Dinner was on the table, and Kaylee was busy telling her adventure as if there'd been nothing wrong with it, her attitude as bubbly as always. Noah, on the other hand, was wound tight as a clock. Or more like a time bomb.

Conversation lagged, and Sierra searched for a way to break the silence.

"Sierra has decided to leave," Noah said, taking matters into his own hands.

"You can't leave," Kaylee cried out. "You promised to watch me race and go to the ball."

"I did, and I still will," Sierra reassured her. "I'm leaving right after the ball."

"Goody. I mean...wait, why do you have to leave at all? I thought you liked it here?" Kaylee frowned as if suddenly realizing Sierra might be leaving for good.

"I thought the same," Laura chimed in, glancing back and forth between her and Noah.

"She's not going anywhere," Tank said, his frown matching Kaylee's. "Sierra means after Thanksgiving. That's what she told me earlier, right before we started searching."

"That's what I planned, but my dad is pretty adamant. He wants me home with the family for the holiday." Not to mention, to interview for a job he'd lined up. The timing was right to get out of the service, and the insurance business was a safe job to his way of thinking. To her, it was a place she couldn't cause problems.

She'd never felt overly welcome at home and staying here would be a close second after everything that had transpired. This was Tank's family, and she'd only borrowed them temporarily. Her time was up.

Tank shook his head. "I'm not sure what cockamamie excuse you want to concoct to make this right, but I'm not buying it. You forget, Sergeant Winters, I know you."

"You do, but you don't know everything about me." No one did. Noah had come the closest, but then even he didn't have all the facts.

Chapter Fifteen

T HE TENSION IN THE room increased with each passing second. By the time Kaylee and Sierra excused themselves, Noah was ready to get out of Dodge himself. It was difficult to balance his feelings when his love for his daughter blinded him, but the voice of reason lay just beneath the surface.

Noah stood to leave, picking up his plate to take it to the sink and make a clean exit.

"Sit down, Noah." His mother's crisp voice brooked no opposition.

"I've got to check on Kaylee." It was an excuse, but a good one.

"She can wait a few minutes." An excuse his mother clearly saw right through.

Noah did as he was told and sat. Bruce leaned back in his chair to get comfortable but didn't say a word. His brother didn't want to miss his mother's obvious reprimand, judging by the tone of her voice. Growing up, it had always been the same, except it was usually Noah who watched his brother get into trouble time after time.

"You know as well as I do that children explore. I get that you're upset. But, Noah, your reactions are born of fear, not sound reasoning. Adults do their best, but no one's perfect. And Sierra's not to blame." Her facial expression softened in understanding, but he knew she wouldn't let this one go.

"How can you say that? She wasn't watching her when she should have been. Instead, she was consorting with him." He nodded toward Bruce, who's expression suddenly darkened.

"Leave me out of it. We talked. So what? It's not a crime," he said defensively.

"It is if it causes someone to lose sight of what's important. Kaylee could have been kidnapped, or attacked by a wild animal, or fallen into the river, or had any number of other awful things happen to her." They didn't understand. It was his job to keep her safe. His ex-wife had left him full responsibility, and he was doing his best, but it clearly wasn't good enough.

"But she wasn't hurt, and now you need to re-set your emotional gauge to flow with reality." His mother's firm voice reminded him of when he and his brother had gotten into a fight as youngsters. It wasn't the last fight, but it was the last time she'd found out about one.

"What you fail to realize is that no one can be perfect all of the time. For example, what about when you come home from the store and are unloading the truck? Who's watching Kaylee? Or when you're in the bathroom, and there's no one else home. Who's watching Kaylee? The list goes on. There are always moments a child is left alone. All it takes is seconds for a child to wander off if they get distracted, and in this case, break the rules. Rules you've set to protect her. If anyone's to blame, it's Kaylee."

The truth of her words gutted him. He was guilty as charged. Kaylee was an active child, and part of keeping her safe meant keeping tabs on her, yes, but it also meant teaching her right and wrong. This time, she had made a wrong turn.

Noah let out a deep breath. "You made your point."

"Good. Then fix the situation. You know what you need to do." Mothers always did seem to know best, but it didn't stop it from irking him.

"Yes, Mom. I'm not fifteen anymore and can figure that part out without motherly input."

"Fine. But I'm still your mother, and it's my prerogative to make sure you do it." The twinkle in her eyes was a sure sign he'd been forgiven. If only Sierra would be of like mind and afford him the same gracious forgiveness.

Yes, he'd apologize, but he wanted to do more than that. Judging by the stiff set of her shoulders when she'd left the room, his bullheadedness may have cost him any chance of moving out of the friend zone with Sierra. But that didn't mean they couldn't still be friends.

Bruce and his mother left him sitting there alone to ponder his next move, but he couldn't think of anything. *Apology first, reparations later.*

Noah went to find Sierra, but she'd retired for the evening. He tapped on her door, determined to set things right.

"Who is it?" she called out.

"Noah. I'd like to talk."

"I think you've said plenty for one night," she admonished, her steely voice not giving him an inch.

"Please?" He was surprised when the door opened.

She stepped back, turned, and went to sit on the edge of the bed. "Say your piece, and then say good night. I'm tired." Sierra yawned, whether for effect or real, he wasn't sure.

He watched her run the brush through her hair repeatedly and gave up waiting for her to make eye contact. "I wanted to say I'm sorry. I was wrong to snap at you."

Her hand paused mid-stroke. "You weren't wrong. That's the problem. I'm the problem, and it's why I'm clearing out after the jubilee. Let's just leave it at that and move on. I told you before that I wasn't family material, and now I've proven it today."

"Today proves nothing. It's something that could happen on my watch, too, and I consider myself a good parent. My mother made me see the error of my ways in blaming you. Sierra, I was afraid, and I let my fear get in the way of good sense and fair play. Try to understand. This isn't about you, honestly."

"Thanks. But it doesn't change anything." She shrugged and looked away as she resumed her brushing, the strokes brisker than before.

Noah couldn't help feeling he needed to prove her wrong. He didn't want what happened to determine Sierra's future. He was sure she had a lot of love to give someone, including a child. And that's when an idea hit him like a brick upside the head in a tornado. He knew what he could do to prove his forgiveness.

"Listen, the day after tomorrow, my mother and Bruce have appointments that can't be changed. I need someone to watch Kaylee after school. It would be great if you could do it."

Sierra shook her head. "I know what you're trying to do, and I appreciate it. It's not that easy, because I've not forgiven myself, no matter whether you have or not. Besides, I've got to work at Whispering Pines from two to six that day."

"Then I'll have someone drop her off after school there and she can be with you. She loves it over there, and she's a good rider. Chad won't mind, I promise." He hadn't been able to take her to Whispering Pines lately, and this was the perfect opportunity to make it happen.

"But still—"

"No buts. Just say yes." It was a brilliant idea.

"I guess. At least there'll be plenty of people to help keep an eye on her, so you won't have to worry."

"I'm not worried." It was true, although convincing Sierra of that was proving more difficult than he'd thought.

Two days went by too fast, her work with the children and horses keeping Sierra busy. The truce between her and Noah was working, keeping them on even footing as friends. It went a long way to calming things down in the Jackson household.

She'd already taken the *GiddyUp Kids* out for rides earlier today. This afternoon, there was a more advanced group of kids coming out for lessons. Chad trusted that she could manage the more experienced group alone, which went a long way to making her feel better about being there. Like she fit in. It was a small step, but it felt good.

She liked working here, and she liked Chad and Amy Andrews. She'd earned their trust the old-fashioned way, and she intended to keep it.

Amy Andrews arrived at the ranch, an excited Kaylee in tow. Noah had arranged for the woman to pick his daughter up from school and deliver her into Sierra's keeping.

"Miss Sierra, I'm here," Kaylee called out, running up to meet her. The other kids from the more experienced class were here already, everyone saddled up and ready to ride.

"I see that, and we've got you all set up with Ginger today. Go see Mr. Chad, and he'll get you fixed up, and then we'll be on our way." She ruffled the girl's hair affectionately and smiled.

"Gotcha," she said as she took off running.

"She was a non-stop chatterbox about the ride today. She kept telling me to go faster so everyone wouldn't leave without her." Amy shook her head and laughed.

"Not a chance. It was all Kaylee's talked about for two days since her dad told her the plan."

"It's a pleasant change for her. She should do it more often. Anyway, have a nice ride." Amy always seemed so settled and happy, and it was something Sierra couldn't help but like and admire. And want.

Happiness.

"Thanks. See you later." Sierra waved and headed for her horse at the front of the group. Six kids waited eagerly, and Kaylee made it seven. It wasn't long before they were on their way, Kaylee settling in toward the middle of the group with Megan, one of her friends from school.

Sierra followed the trail toward the river, the direction pre-decided upon with Chad. It was a newer trail and would be more of a challenge for the kids, but it was a terrific way for advanced students to gain more experience. She kept turning around to check on the kids, mindful they were following the rules and staying on the trail. Spread out, the group looked more like an endless caravan than a class.

Thirty minutes into the ride, she came to the fork that would lead toward the river. It was a beautiful trail, and one Chad worked on to clean up over the past few days. She went a little way ahead, and then stopped, turning back to watch the kids as they rounded the corner.

Without warning, Kaylee shot to the left, heading straight for Sierra at a fast pace, grim determination on the girl's face. "Kaylee, stop," she called out, watching as she barreled toward a downed tree.

Sierra waved her arms. "Stop, the log—"

Kaylee leaned forward just as she reached the log. Seconds turned into milliseconds as time seemed to slow. The horse sailed over the obstacle in his path, and Kaylee wore a look of surprise as she was unseated, flew, and landed with a rolling thud.

"Children stay put," Sierra hollered as she raced to reach Kaylee.

Sierra slid off her horse and hobbled to Kaylee as fast as she could, ignoring the pain shooting down her leg. "I'm here, honey," she said, checking Kaylee's head for signs of injury and then her limbs. She wanted to pick Kaylee up, hold her tightly, and say a prayer of thanks she hadn't been injured. Or killed.

She shoved back images of another time and place when a soldier hadn't been so lucky, needing to focus on Kaylee. The screaming pain in her leg forced her to sit by Kaylee's side and wait, hoping it would subside soon so she could be of use.

Kaylee sat up. "Did you see me?" Not at all the first words Sierra had expected.

"I did. Didn't you see the log? Are you okay?" Sierra asked, trying to make sure Kaylee wasn't hurt.

"I'm fine. It's just a little fall. I wanted to tell you something and thought it would be easier to take a shortcut." Kaylee used the same wide-eyed innocent look she'd used on her father. Sierra was beginning to think kids learned the art of manipulation in a manual or a class at school.

"You scared the life right out of me. You haven't trained to jump, and it was dangerous." It was a total understatement. The truth of how Sierra really felt as Kaylee flew wasn't something a seven-year-old needed to hear. Not if she ever wanted her to ride a horse again.

Kaylee pulled a pout. "I'm sorry. It looked so easy. The log didn't look that big from where I was sitting." She shook her head and frowned.

"You shouldn't have broken the line. You know the rules." Sierra couldn't help the firmness in her voice, even though what she really wanted to do was hug her tightly. They had rules at the Whispering

Pines, and Kaylee had broken them. Rules kept the kids safe.

"I just wanted to tell you something," Kaylee whined, the pout on her face deepening. At her age, she didn't understand all the adult fuss.

Chad would have a cow.

And Noah would be worse.

Sierra would rather be anywhere than here when he found out. She could almost hear the accusation and disappointment in their voices now, most of which would be directed squarely at Sierra. "We need to cancel the rest of the ride and return to the barn so we can get you checked out just to be sure."

The kids all groaned and sent frustrated glances at Kaylee, but at least they didn't say anything.

"But I'm fine," Kaylee whined again.

Sierra shook her head. "Sorry. I'm not a doctor, and Dr. Duncan will be the judge of that."

Kaylee tried to stand but looked a little shaky. "Where's Ginger?"

Sierra helped her up as best she could, trying not to put a lot of weight on her bad leg. It would be disastrous if they both toppled over. "One of the other kids will round her up. You're riding back with me just in case you took a harder fall than you seem to think." They'd have to ride double with her securely in front of Sierra. The last thing she needed was for a jittery girl or a possible unknown injury to make things worse.

"Seriously? I'm not a baby." Kaylee stood there, hands on her hips, her lower lip trembling.

"Riding with this advanced group was a special favor from Chad. Don't make this worse by trying to shrug it off as nothing. There are consequences for breaking the rules. Let's do this my way. Please," Sierra added softly, praying the little girl wouldn't actually have a temper tantrum or some version of a hissy fit right here with everyone watching.

Kaylee looked as though she had a thing or two to say about Sierra's decision but thought better of it. "Yes, ma'am," she mumbled.

"Jeremy, can you give Kaylee a hand and help her up in front of me after I get mounted?

"Sure thing, Miss Sierra." The older boy slid off his horse, tying the reins to a tree.

"And, Angel, grab Ginger's reins and lead her back to the barn, please."

"Yes, Miss Sierra." Angel turned and headed straight for where Ginger stood munching grass by the trees.

"Give me a minute to call Mr. Andrews first so that he can notify Mr. Jackson." The kids had all gathered around to keep a watchful eye on what was happening, the looks of frustration lining most of their faces only growing deeper with each minute that passed. They weren't any happier with the ride being cut short than Kaylee.

"Do you have to tell him?" Kaylee asked.

"Of course, he's responsible for all of you. And so am I. By the way, what is it you wanted to tell me?"

"I thought I saw a fox, and I wanted you to see it. I was going to ask if the horses would be afraid?" "Oh, honey. It was a great question, just a lousy outcome. But, no, the foxes won't alarm the horses. They are much bigger, and a fox isn't looking to pick a fight with them. A bear would be far more of a concern, but I don't think there are any around Whispering Pines."

"Okay, good to know," Kaylee said, her voice totally lacking her typical upbeat attitude.

Sierra turned away to make the call, needing privacy for what she had to tell Chad. His concern was obvious but not frantic, giving her some small measure of reassurance after they talked. By the time they arrived, both the doctor and Noah would be there. She could only hope Noah would take the same approach as Chad.

Fat chance.

Sierra had failed again. When would she learn? Three strikes, and two of them concerning Noah and Kaylee.

I'm out.

Chapter Sixteen

♥

THE SPEED LIMIT WASN'T high enough, at least, not on this trip back to Hallbrook. Noah passed a slow-moving tractor and edged his speedometer higher, anxious to get to Whispering Pines. Chad's call informing him of Kaylee's fall had taken ten years off his life. After getting someone to cover his patients for the rest of the day, he'd left, needing to get to his little girl. It was the only surefire way to be reassured she was truly okay, something Chad couldn't make him feel over the phone.

Especially considering the doc hadn't seen or examined her yet. All the way to the ranch, the doctor's words rang in his head. *Sierra was leading the children...* Noah's brain seemed stuck on that one piece of information. He'd entrusted Kaylee to her, hoping to set things straight between them. But the opposite had occurred. It seemed everything terrible happening to Kaylee lately, involved Sierra in some fashion.

Kaylee was only seven, but she was a good rider. He couldn't begin to think of what had gone wrong. He didn't want to blame Sierra, but she was in charge of the kids on the ride and therefore the one responsible for their safety. A sense of deja vu hit him. It was only days ago he'd felt this same fear for Kaylee.

Noah pulled into the driveway that led up to the ranch and drove to the top of the hill. Jumping out of the truck, he raced over to where Dr. Duncan stood watching him approach. "I thought they'd be back by now. Where are they?"

"Relax, Noah. She'll be fine. Sierra reassured us she wasn't injured. Checking her over is a formality. There they are now. See for yourself." He pointed across the field to where he saw a long line of kids and their horses headed this way, Sierra at the lead with Kaylee sitting in front of her. His stomach clenched tighter, his worry going into overdrive. If Sierra hadn't thought Kaylee well enough to ride back to the barn by herself, she must have some concerns.

Noah raced to meet them, and Sierra pulled up on the reins to stop her horse.

"Daddy, you didn't have to come and get me. I'm fine," Kaylee said in disgust. Not exactly what he'd expected to hear after rushing to her side. The fall hadn't curbed her tongue or her attitude.

"Of course, I did. That's what daddies do." He held up his arms, expecting Sierra to help her out of the saddle so Noah could check her over.

"I'm so sorry, Noa—"

"Later, Sierra." He cut her off because checking Kaylee's injuries were more important than any discussion. He ran a hand down each of her arms and legs, his heart breaking at the tiny cuts on her skin and the bruise already starting to form. "Does anything hurt when I press on it? Or move it?"

"No. I keep telling you that. I'm fine. It's not like I haven't fallen before." Kaylee squirmed to get out of his arms. "Put me down. I'm not a baby."

"You'll always be my baby. And when you fell before, it was off a pony in a pen. Big difference," Noah said, not about to give in to her big girl demands.

Dr. Duncan joined him and began to check her vitals. Noah let him take over, knowing he was the doctor in charge.

"Not to me. I just hate all the big kids who saw it. I'm sure they're laughing at me. Or mad." She snuck a glance in their direction.

"Why would they be mad?" he asked, frowning. The idea of the kids mad at his daughter for an accident didn't seem fair.

"'Cause I ruined the trip," she said dejectedly.

"It's not your fault. Accidents happen." Except they happened more often when whoever was in charge wasn't paying attention. He recalled the moment he'd see Sierra talking to Bruce. Her lax vigilance then had caused the problem, allowing Kaylee to wander off alone. Noah was positive this would be the same issue.

"Yes, it is. I got out of the line and left the trail, trying to take a shortcut. And then there was this log. More like a tree. And Ginger, well, she jumped. Only I couldn't stay on," Kaylee said, shrugging as if it were no big deal.

Noah's gut clenched, knowing the outcome could have been tragic if she'd hit her head or landed on her back. "You jumped? But you've never done that before. People have to train to learn how."

"I know, Daddy, and that's why I want to learn. It was awesome flying through the air—at least until I fell off." Kaylee grinned.

"She seems right as rain, Noah. Take her home, give her a hot bath for her sore muscles, and she'll be fine. Clearly, Kaylee hasn't lost the ability to see the humor in the situation, and I'm not concerned she hit her head. She seems on point to me." The doctor grinned, his comment directed at Kaylee's insane remark about flying after being tossed to the ground.

"Thank, Doc." His mother may have talked him into giving Sierra a pass the first time around, but this time, there was no way. Sierra should have been watching the kids. All of them.

He picked Kaylee up and headed for the truck, not bothering to talk to Sierra. The problem was Noah no longer knew what to say. The only thing he knew for sure was that he needed her gone.

Noah drove off without another word. His attitude was expected, but still, the reality wasn't easy to swallow. They were like a round peg and square hole when it came to dealing with one another. Normally, she wouldn't care what he thought, but Noah was one of the few people whose opinion she did care about.

"Don't worry about Noah, he'll get over himself soon enough. He's a bit overprotective of Kaylee," Chad said, shaking his head watching Noah's trail of dust as he departed.

"He has every right to be upset. I oversaw the ride, and it was my job to keep everyone safe. I blew it." Sierra let out a deep sigh.

"Hogwash. Kids will be kids, and in this case, Kaylee broke the rules. You can't put kids in a cocoon and expect them to learn and grow," the doctor said, reassuring her. It helped, but it didn't diminish the sting of Noah's rejection.

"It's been a long morning. Why don't you head back to the Jackson place and go talk to Noah? You look like you lost your best friend, and the kids and I can take care of brushing down the horses and turning them out." Chad was going the extra mile to help her get through this, but he didn't understand.

"I don't know." She shrugged. She did know though, and she didn't like what she knew. This was the second incident with Kaylee, and there was no avoiding the truth, she wasn't good with kids.

"Go." Chad gave her a nudge in the general direction of her car.

"Fine. I can see I'm not wanted." Her comment was only partly teasing. She liked and respected both men, but so far, she'd done nothing to earn theirs. Even more reason to return to military life, where she knew the rules, knew what to do, and did it well. At least, most of the time. Sierra was no longer sure she could stay until after the jubilee.

"You know that's not true. You've always got a place here. The kids love you, and I don't think we could have found a better person to help us out."

"Thanks, Chad." She meant it. Sometimes a person just needed to hear the words. "I'll see you tomorrow." *But what if it happens again?* The seed of doubt had been planted, making her question whether she would return. More than likely, she'd be home by tomorrow.

"Okay." She turned to the kids. "And thank you, everyone, for your help and understanding. I'm sorry your ride got cut short, but we'll make it up to you, I promise." The last two words slipped out before Sierra could call them back. How could she promise something she wasn't sure she could deliver?

Sierra drove back to the Jackson ranch, unable to get the image of Kaylee flying off the horse scene out of her head. Fear for the little girl had sent her adrenaline into a raging spike, one that pushed her closer to the edge of a relapse.

Her sense of dread eased when she didn't see Noah's truck parked in front of the house. Perhaps he'd taken Kaylee for ice cream as a treat after her troubles. It would certainly make things easier for her to do what she needed to do.

Leave.

And with any luck, she'd be gone before Noah returned.

Sierra entered the house and headed for the kitchen, almost positive she'd find Laura there. "Good afternoon, Laura. Do you know where Noah and Kaylee got off too? She took a tumble off a horse today, and I was hoping to see how she's doing."

"Oh, dear. Noah didn't tell you?" Laura's words caught her off guard, and she was trying to refocus.

"Tell me what?"

"Kaylee said her arm was hurting, and Noah being Noah, rushed her straight to Lancaster to get it X-rayed at his hospital. If you ask me, it's bruised. If Dr. Duncan didn't reckon anything is wrong, chances are there isn't. Not to mention Noah's own assessment matched the doctors. But Noah's hard-headed when it comes to my granddaughter, in case you haven't noticed, and he's worried something might have been missed."

"I did notice. Let's just hope you're right, and it's a simple case of overprotective. I feel awful about the whole thing. In fact, I've decided to go home before anything worse happens. I'm not good with kids, and the last thing I want to do is have someone get hurt on my account. Especially a child." She'd come to the final decision on the drive back to the Jackson ranch. Her promise to the children would have to be fulfilled by Chad, something she was confident the man would oblige.

"That's ridiculous, and you know it. The kids at Whispering Pines love you. Chad told me all about it. Shame you'd run from the good you're doing." Laura returned her gaze to the vegetables she was chopping like it was a foregone conclusion that Sierra would come to her senses and stay.

The older woman was wrong. "Kaylee getting hurt isn't good. I'd tally that into the bad column. My mom and dad are pushing for me to come home anyway." It was the truth, even if it was an excuse.

"Sounds like you're running away." This time, Laura stopped chopping. Her gaze bore into Sierra as if trying to see deep into her soul. "Maybe it's time you stopped. I think you've done well here, both physically and mentally. It doesn't take much to see you have a lot going on, stuff you won't talk about, but I've got eyes in my head and can see a positive change."

"You're right, I do have a lot going on. I appreciate you opening your home to me the way you did —but I do need to leave. I'll pack up my things and run to the barn to see Tank. Can you tell Noah and Kaylee goodbye for me? Oh, and make sure Kaylee knows I'll be at the jubilee. A promise is a promise."

Sierra might not be good for much else right now, but she would always honor her promises.

Noah Jackson was a good man. So were all the other people she'd met recently. They were good people based on their hearts and not deeds done for others. Something Sierra didn't understand. It was deeds that proved a person's worth and gave measure to achievements. But the love they showed for one another based on heart, only made her feel increasingly like an outsider. Different in a way she wasn't sure she could overcome. Her life has always been about doing deeds. And when it came to deeds, she'd done nothing but fail since the bombing in Afghanistan.

Deal with the past.

The thought was crystal clear and came out of nowhere, a good indicator God was watching over her. She wasn't alone in her struggle. It was time to head home, but not for the reasons she'd told Laura. It was time for Sierra to figure her life out, to figure out what mattered. Including her future.

First, she needed to figure out the past, which meant talking to the one man who would have some answers she'd waited all her life to hear.

Her father.

Chapter Seventeen

♥

NOAH WALKED IN THE house, a tired and half-asleep Kaylee in his arms. After dropping her off in her room and helping to get her ready for bed, he tucked her in. "Night, sweetheart."

"I love you, Daddy. I'm sorry I broke the rules today." Kaylee yawned and rubbed her eyes.

Brushing her hair back off her face, he chucked his daughter's chin. "Okay, honey. But in the future, remember rules are good to follow, and they can help keep you safe." Not to mention, keep him heart healthy.

"But I'm okay. My arm looks like the time I fell off the swing. Remember, Daddy?"

Boy, did he. "I do. That was another not-so- favorite day." He smiled and leaned over to drop a kiss on her forehead. "Sleep tight."

"Night, Daddy." Kaylee pulled the comforter up under her chin, snuggled tight, and rolled on her side.

Noah turned out the light and walked out the door. The problem with what his daughter mentioned was that the swing-set incident had been on his watch. Proof he wasn't infallible when it came to Kaylee. He'd been a fool and owed Sierra an apology. Again.

When would he learn? He headed straight for the kitchen, surprised by the quiet.

"I'm guessing you've gone and done it again." He wasn't even fully through the kitchen door when his mother spoke, making him wonder who she was talking to. He looked around, but no one else was there.

Noah frowned. "Who's done what, Mom?"

"You. She's gone. And I think you're the reason. I know how you can be about Kaylee." His mother wasn't making any sense, but whatever she was carrying on about couldn't be good, judging by the tone of her voice.

"Who's gone? Sierra?"

"Of course, Sierra. Who else would I be talking about? What did you say to her?" He hadn't said anything. How could Sierra leaving be his fault? And more importantly, where had she gone?

He'd been a bear, yes, but it didn't make sense for her to leave. His lack of communication couldn't possibly be the only thing that had driven her away.

I'm not good with kids. Her words drifted in the recesses of his brain. He'd done nothing but reinforce what she thought with his silence. Well, silence and cutting her off as she tried to apologize.

Noah sat in the chair and rubbed the back of his neck. It had been a long day, and it still wasn't over. "I need to apologize to her. My only excuse is that I was worried. Call it being overprotective or whatever you want, but I took Kaylee to the hospital to make sure she was okay. So where did Sierra go?"

"Home. Are you happy? You worried needlessly after Dr. Duncan told you she was fine. You're a nurse and you knew she was fine. But you doubted everyone, including yourself, letting your worry get the better of you."

"Without an X-ray, there was no way to be certain there wasn't a fracture. As to Sierra, you mean home to Boston? Or back to the base? And did she mention anything about coming back? Like for the Veteran's Day events. Kaylee will hate me if she thinks Sierra's gone and isn't coming back to watch her in the race because of me."

"She said to tell you both goodbye and to tell Kaylee she'll be at the jubilee. A promise is a promise. Too bad you didn't promise to be fair. I liked having Sierra around, and the kids at Whispering Pines love her. It's not just Kaylee who lost her. We all did." The stubborn set of his mother's jaw was proof he'd crossed a line in her books.

Noah let out a deep sigh. His mother didn't know it, but he would miss Sierra the most. The deep ache knowing she was gone wasn't just because he'd wronged her, it was because he'd been falling in love. And now, he'd lost his second chance at love out of stupidity.

Or he'd pushed her away out of fear.

One thing he knew for sure—a text, email, or phone call, wasn't going to fix things. He'd landed deep in the manure pile this time, and it would take far more than words to make things right. Action was the one thing that would speak loud enough that Sierra wouldn't ignore him.

Find her heart's desire.

Rhaegar.

Working at the VA hospital didn't come without benefits, and this was the best reason ever to call in a few favors. Of course, he'd try and pull off a feat even Sierra hadn't been able to manage. And knowing Sierra, she'd pulled out all the stops. He could only hope his contacts proved more effective than hers.

All the way home, Sierra tried to figure out what to say to her dad. Knowing the conversation with her father was long overdue, didn't make it any easier to prepare for. The colonel didn't like anyone calling him out—on anything. One simply listened and obeyed, never challenged.

That was about to change. He was her father, not her boss. The front door opened, and her mother stepped out on the porch, a look of happy surprise on her face. Sierra slid out of the car and went into her mother's waiting arms.

"I'm so glad you're home. You didn't call to let me know you were coming." She pulled Sierra close for a hug.

"Hi, Mom. It was a last-minute decision." *Literally.*

"Your father will be pleased. He's been in a mood ever you insisted you weren't coming home for Thanksgiving." Talking a mile a minute, her mother's warm smile touched Sierra's heart.

Laura was right, and there was some healing going on inside of Sierra, because for once, she didn't want to turn tail and run. The rest would depend how the colonel responded to her request for a meeting and to the subject matter.

"Well, well. My prodigal daughter has returned. How's the leg?" The colonel's deep voice and no-nonsense comment made her tense. It was always the same. The man didn't express feelings or have meaningless discussions.

"Hey there. Not sure how long I'll be staying. Leg's doing better, and I'll be returning to the base soon." She could be just as matter of fact as he could be—after all, she'd learned the art of direct conversation from him. Sierra followed him into the house. No hug. No warm welcome. Nothing. More reason this meeting with her father was long overdue.

"Now that you're here, you should plan on sticking around until after Thanksgiving. Your mother will be brokenhearted if you don't."

"Yes, sir. I'll consider it, but I can't promise anything." Conversation first, and the decision how long to stay after that. "I was wondering if you and I could talk."

He stopped in his tracks and turned to face her, brows drawn tight and a questioning expression, but otherwise, he remained silent.

"Privately," Sierra added.

The colonel frowned and glanced at his watch. "Can it wait an hour? I'm watching a football game."

Sierra rolled her eyes and shook her head. It was always the same with him. "That's fine. No, actually, it's not fine." For once, she wanted to be in the driver seat. "I'd like to talk. *Now*. It's important."

"Charles, go talk to your daughter. I'll press the record button, and you can watch it later." Her mother advocating for her was a surprise. Typically, she always sided with the colonel, making sure he got whatever he wanted.

She could tell he wanted to disagree, but a look of resignation crossed his face. It was ridiculous that it almost took an act of Congress to get a private meeting with her own father.

"Let's go into my office, seeing as I'm outnumbered." He shot her mother a half-smile, revealing a couple of dimples. Funny, but she didn't remember them being there at all. Either he never smiled, or she had never paid attention.

"Fine by me." Sierra nodded.

Her mother's sweet and gentle smile softened her features before she turned and walked away, leaving Sierra to follow the colonel down the hall.

He moved behind his oversized mahogany desk and sat in the leather chair, the creaks and squeaks a good indicator of its age. Her father wasn't one for change.

Sierra moved to stand in front of the window, putting a light behind her. It was a tactic she'd learned in the military when wanting to gain an advantage over one's adversary. It made it difficult for the other person to read someone's facial expressions.

"What's on your mind?" he asked, getting straight to the point. Sierra expected nothing less. It felt as though she'd prepared for this moment her entire life.

Sierra let out a deep breath. "You. Me. Us," she forced the words out.

The colonel tensed, but it was the only sign the words had registered. He remained silent, waiting for her to continue. Another tried and true tactic used to control a conversation. But this time, she was ready and had no intention of falling in line with the normal flow.

"I'm dealing with some issues, and one of the main ones happens to revolve around you. All my life, I've looked up to you and wanted to make you proud of me. You wanted me to be a girlie girl with all the fancy frills. But that's not who I am. It's why I try so hard at everything I do, wanting to finally earn your respect. But I've concluded it's not possible."

"Sierra," he interrupted, his voice deep and commanding, but she held up her hand. Not this time. He wouldn't stop her.

"Let me finish," she said, surprised when he complied. It was like finally saying the words locked in her heart for so long lifted a weight off her chest. There was much to be said, and now that she'd started, she was more than ready to get it all off her chest.

"I wanted your love and your respect, and I don't think it's too much to ask of my own father. You were never my commanding officer, and I'm tired of feeling like I don't fit—with you. I want to hear from you, no-holds-barred, what it is about me that you can't handle. I'm your daughter, and I'm a soldier. That should account for something." She let out another deep breath. There was more she could say, but rehashing the past would serve no good, and saying anything else would be restating what she'd already said. Another tactic she'd learned in the military. *Know when to shut up.*

Her father rubbed a hand over his face and forehead, clearly agitated with the discussion. Another tidbit she'd learned over the year was he who speaks first loses. She'd presented her side and wouldn't speak another word, no matter how long he took to answer.

The silence was deafening; her heart on the other hand, was pounding loud and hard.

The colonel stood, his shoulders slumped, and his face an expression of pain. "Sierra, you must know I never wanted you to join the military."

It was nothing more than she'd expected to hear. But knowing the truth and finally hearing it were two different things. He'd never come right out and admitted it to her face, and it hurt worse than she'd expected. "Who doesn't know? You've never been quiet about your position regarding women in the military, especially me. Trust me, I know your feelings on the subject."

The colonel looked surprised, but not happy. "It's not what you think. The especially-you part is because you're my daughter, but you've misunderstood my reasoning. There's no disputing my opinion on the subject. I lobbied against it and still do, but it's not because I think women aren't capable. It's because the thought of losing my own daughter tears me into tiny little pieces. I fear they'd be pieces I couldn't put together again." His voice broke, sounding old and tired.

What was he talking about? It sounded more like a diversion tactic. An exceptionally good one. She needed to stay focused, not wanting to dissect the emotions behind his words.

"You always wanted me to dress like a girl, act like a girl, be a girl. The truth is women are in the military. We earn the right to be there every day, fighting for our country, and defending our honor. We breathe the same air as men and can be trained to excel the same as men. Any weakness is because of men holding us back or women who don't belong. But there are men who fall into the same category." She crossed the room, placing her palms on his desk and leaning in toward him. "Not everyone is cut out to be a soldier, but it has nothing to do with their gender."

His hand covered hers. "The reason I wanted you to be interested in feminine things growing up was out of fear you'd want to be like your old man. I didn't want to see that happen. Everything I did was to keep you from choosing a military life. Clearly, I failed."

Sierra drew back, his words more upsetting than she'd expected. What girl didn't want to feel loved and protected by her father? But what he was saying now certainly wasn't the message she'd gotten growing up. "And yet here I am in the military. It's my life. I've worked hard to get where I'm at, and not once have you given me accolades or an atta girl for my achievements. I'm over it. I'm tired of fighting for you to love and respect me. To be proud of me." The well-rehearsed lines came across lacking after his explanation. But she'd been blindsided.

"You've got it all wrong, sweetheart. I've always respected what you do. I've followed your career closely over the years and couldn't be prouder."

"Then why not tell me?" This was the million-dollar question Sierra had wanted answered for a lifetime.

"Because if I did, you might stay in longer, and I never wanted you to join. I'm not afraid of much, but I'm afraid of losing you. Sierra, I love you." He took her by the hand and pulled her into his arms, but not before she saw a glimmer of tears in his eyes.

She'd finally broken the colonel into showing emotion, but it didn't feel like a win. Hearing him say he loved her...well, that did. "To me, following in your footsteps was the right thing to do. And I don't regret it. I love what I do most of the time." She smiled and wiped away the tears that rolled down her cheeks. Showing emotion wasn't something that came easily.

"Rhaegar always kept me safe, and I'm sure I'll be assigned another great dog to work with. Or it's time to take on more responsibility and move up the ladder. Take after my old man." She used his own words against him, surprised at how easy it felt to talk with all the masks ripped away and the real man exposed before her. "As long as it's not a desk job. I'm not sure I could be tied to an office."

"A desk job is what I wanted for you, honestly. I prayed every night for God to bring you home safely. It was the only thing I could do to help protect you after you enlisted. Everything I've said and done may not have been right, but you're my daughter, and protecting you was my most important mission."

"I get it. I just wish you'd explained. I feel like so much time has been wasted. You were always the colonel, with high demands and rarely satisfied. I always thought I was one huge disappointment." The colonel wasn't one to talk much, and she'd learned the fine art of evasion from him. It was time for them to find a new way to communicate, a medium ground that paved the way for a better relationship—one filled with honesty.

He stepped back and walked to the window as if lost deep in thought. He turned to face her. "I'm an old man and set in my ways. My job demanded me to be tough, and I'm sorry if I couldn't separate home and work as well as I'd intended. Especially knowing how much it hurt you. After I found the army men you stashed under your bed, I knew in my heart I'd lost the battle to steer you clear of the military, but it didn't stop me from trying."

"Wait, you knew?" she asked. The day was full of surprises.

The colonel smiled and nodded. "Of course, I did. It was my job to know everything," he said, shooting her a playful wink.

All these years, and she'd had no idea. Even now, it was hard to grasp the full impact. The colonel had been trying to protect her. The same way Noah was trying to protect Kaylee. And honestly, it was the same way when she'd teamed up with Rhaegar. She would have done anything to protect him, and he to protect her. An unbreakable bond.

And that was the reason she had to find her canine companion.

It was also the reason she shouldn't have walked away from Noah. Half in love with him, she'd run away when she should have stayed to help him understand. No one ever said relationships were easy, she and her father were proof of that. But the issue with Noah ran deeper.

She had to report back to duty in early December, and Sierra wouldn't make promises she couldn't keep. Which included any form of a promise to Noah and Kaylee for a safe return if she were sent to war again. There was no way she could put her life on the line and give it her all, knowing there was someone back home counting on her to return.

Chapter Eighteen

♥

IN BETWEEN WORK AND making calls trying to find Rhaegar, Noah had stayed busy. Working on the house wasn't even a possibility at this point. Showing Sierra how important she was to him was his top priority. And even that had to be interrupted by Halloween and the church's Bobbing for Apples Kid's Night.

Of course, Kaylee had gone as a princess, claiming it was a trial run for the ball. He would have agreed with her if she hadn't dressed as a princess for the last four years. After Sierra had dubbed her royalty, his daughter's focus on her princess role had intensified to a whole new level.

Coffee in hand, Noah moved to the living room to settle in with his laptop and notebook. More research and more calls were on his agenda this morning as he took advantage of Kaylee being in school and him having a day off from work.

"Morning, Noah. Are you going to help me out today on the ranch?" Bruce asked as he headed for the door with a thermos in hand.

"Sorry. I've got to find Rhaegar, and the jubilee is coming up quick. My window of opportunity is closing to make a grand gesture, and I think after the way I acted, grand is the only thing that will get Sierra's attention." The general family consensus was that he'd royally blown it, and not a day went by they didn't remind him of that fact.

"Maybe just lay out all your cards and beg for forgiveness." Bruce had been the quietest about the ordeal, not that he hadn't put in his two cents. That was one more thing Noah regretted about Sierra's departure. Bruce had been coming out of whatever held him bound to the past, but his progress had stalled after she left.

"That worked the first time around. I'm not so sure it'll be enough the second." Over the past week, Noah had finally let himself admit the truth about Sierra. He needed another chance to prove to her what she meant to him, and that he wanted her in his life. He'd share her with the military if that's what it took, but most importantly, when she came home, he wanted it to be to him.

"There is that," Bruce said, moving closer. "You were an idiot."

"Tell me something I don't know." Noah shook his head and let out a heavy sigh.

"I reckon you need some help. The reason Sierra tries so hard and thinks she needs to be perfect is because of the colonel. All she ever wanted was his respect and to prove to him she's capable. She wants him to be proud of who she is and what she's chosen to do with her life. Her accomplishments." It was the most his brother had said at one time...in a long time. "I shouldn't be telling you any of this, but I can't stand to see you moping around."

"It's not moping. It's called thinking. And I already know about her father. She said as much in different words."

"Then try this on for size. When we served together, it wasn't uncommon for the male soldiers to take her presence as a challenge to their masculinity. They competed against her and went to great pains to beat her—in everything. I told you before about the one time, but it happened far more often than you can imagine. Sierra rose to the challenges, punishing herself with grueling PT workouts every chance she got. She hates to lose because, to her, it equates to her being a failure. It's the same with the explosion in Afghanistan. She blames herself and thinks it's all her fault. Mistakes are failures—which she equates with a loss of respect. And respect is something she's worked hard for all her life with the colonel as a father."

Noah cringed. "Now that I didn't know. She never said a word."

"Of course not. Sierra's a private person, but sometimes hunkered down in a bunker, soldiers talk. Especially soldiers who become loyal friends. In the dark of the night, innermost secrets are shared, and by mutual agreement, never discussed after. I'm only telling you all this now because I genuinely believe you care about her, and that she cares about you. Although, Lord knows why." Bruce grinned at his own joke.

"Ha-ha, wise guy. Thanks for telling me. I hate that I contributed to her feeling like a failure with Kaylee or at Whispering Pines. That wasn't my intention." He'd known the truth, but not how deep the truth ran. It made him regret his actions even more now.

"Neither was it anyone's intention from our platoon, but it happened. Sierra was the one responsible for choosing the path when she came to a fork in the road. She's still blaming herself for the soldier's death and the injuries to others, including mine, hers, and Rhaegar."

"Wow. That's a heavy load to bear." Noah's heart went out to Sierra. "Was there any indicator it was the wrong path? Could she have known?"

"No. And for all we know, the other path was booby-trapped as well. No one will ever know, but it doesn't change the guilt she carries. She did an excellent job protecting everyone the best she could the minute Rhaegar picked up a scent. It just wasn't enough, and it played right into her own self-doubts. She's had a tough go of it."

Noah's heart ached for Sierra now that he knew she was carrying such a heavy burden. He had to find Rhaegar and give her back a piece of herself that she'd lost on that mission. He caught and held his brother's gaze. "Much like you. I'm here to help in any way if you need me. You know that." It was the least he could offer since he'd been the one to run Sierra off.

"I do know it, and thanks. Sierra and I started talking before she left, and it helped. A lot. I'm better now because of her. Hate to see her disappear completely if you know what I mean." Bruce's words only confirmed what Noah had already suspected.

"I do. If we find Rhaegar, wouldn't she be more likely to stick around? I would think she'd need a home base for him. It's not like you can take your pet when you're deployed." And by the sounds of it, her parents won't be high on her list of dog sitters.

Bruce nodded. "That's what I'm thinking. You need to find the dog."

"I'm trying," Noah said, frustrated that his brother didn't seem to understand just how hard he'd been working on it.

"Try harder." Two words that said it all.

He needed help. "What do you suggest I do? You know the ins and outs of the military better than I do. I've used up every resource at my disposal and still no luck." He wasn't sure how much headway Bruce could make either, but it was worth a try.

"All but one."

Noah frowned, his brother's comment baffling. "What do you mean?"

"The colonel. Who better to pull strings and find out what you need to know? And he's her father—should count for something, even if they aren't close." Bruce was right, and it was something he should have thought himself.

Except Sierra wouldn't appreciate him enlisting the aid of her father. That would be crossing the line. But it was a line he was willing to cross under the circumstances. "That's an idea, but one she would hate. Still...it makes sense to try. I met him once and liked the guy. The man commanded respect, something Sierra and I disagree about. I'm sure he'd at least talk to me, and if he can't help, maybe he can steer me in the right direction."

The more he thought about it, the more he liked it. Sierra wouldn't even know he'd talked to the colonel unless he found the dog. And if he did, his methods wouldn't be questioned. "Thanks, Bruce. Great idea." Noah was anxious to act. Time was not on his side.

"You're welcome. Get to it. I've got work to do, and the sooner you find the dog, the sooner you can give me a hand. I do need help running this place, and we're not quite back to a profitable enough point yet where I can hire ranch hands." His brother crossed the room to the front door, signaling the end of their first real discussion in a long time.

"You're doing an excellent job. I know the circumstances of you coming home weren't great, but you were needed here. And Mom is ecstatic to have you back. The ranch is safe."

"Thanks." Bruce looked uncomfortable and exited the house quickly. His brother had a lot to say to Noah about Sierra but talking about himself was another story.

Noah looked up the colonel's number from the business card he'd stashed in his wallet. He dialed and waited, fully expecting voice mail, and trying to decide what to say.

"Winters." The colonel's crisp voice still carried the authority of a man used to being in command.

"Yes, this is Noah Jackson. I'm sorry to bother you, sir, but I'd like to ask you a favor." Knowing what he needed to ask and asking it were too different things. More than likely, he'd only get one shot to convince the colonel to help.

"Am I supposed to know you? How did you get my number?" The colonel's sharp comment was a good indicator the call would end soon if he didn't capture his attention.

"Yes, sir. We met at the symposium at the VA hospital. I joined you for lunch after, and you gave me your card." Noah was sure the colonel met lots of people and handed out lots of cards, but it was worth a try.

"Yes, now I remember. Noah. You're the nurse at the hospital, right?" Of course, that's how he was remembered. A male nurse wasn't common, but Noah didn't mind if that's what it took to keep the old man on the phone and listening.

"Yes, sir. About the favor. I need help finding a dog." Noah fully understood why Sierra struggled to gain ground with the man. His demeanor didn't exactly exude warmth or encourage friendly con-versation.

"And you're calling me because..."

"It's for your daughter." He should have led with that part, but then again, not after what he'd learned from Sierra and Bruce.

"I see. When we met, I wasn't aware you knew my daughter." A hint of question shadowed his voice as it sharpened.

"I didn't. Sierra recently stayed here at our ranch for a couple of weeks."

"With her buddy from the Army is what I heard." Apparently, that's all Sierra had told her parents, considering they weren't close.

"My brother Bruce is her buddy from the military, yes. But she was also here with my mother, my daughter, and me." Noah was quick to squash any imaginative picture the colonel might create in his head that was far from the truth and damaging to Sierra's character.

"I didn't know, but I guess I had that coming since I didn't ask." Noah sensed resignation in the man's voice, the change catching him off guard. "So, I'm guessing you're trying to locate Rhaegar?"

"Yes, sir. And I've exhausted all avenues. I'm trying to surprise Sierra." And win favor in her eyes again but telling the colonel that would lead to questions he didn't want to answer.

"Interesting. Seems above and beyond for the brother of her friend, unless there's more to your motive than simple surprise." The man had zeroed in with exacting efficiency.

Noah knew what he was asking, but how should he answer? "You could say that, sir. I care about your daughter. A lot," he added, settling for the truth. "I've bungled a few things with her and feel the need to make up for them with actions rather than words."

"I like a man of action. Tell me more."

"I've called every rescue center and followed every lead, but I'm getting the same runaround Sier- ra's been getting. I'd hoped my connections at the hospital would help me, but that hasn't been enough to get around the red tape." Every place he called had the same excuses. Lost file. Status unknown. Or there was a mountain of paperwork ahead of his request. Important paperwork. The messages all amounted to the same thing. No one was willing to help.

"And you're hoping my connections can? I'm not in the military anymore, son." The personalized "son" on the end of his remark struck Noah as odd. He hadn't heard the word used in relation to himself in a long time, not since his father died. Truth be told, coming from the colonel, it was quite an honor. "No, but you will always be a colonel in every soldier's eyes in the Army."

"There is that. And seeing as I like you, Noah Jackson, and I love my daughter, I'm going to help you. I haven't always done right by her, so maybe this is a chance for both of us to make amends and show how much we care." The colonel's declaration shocked him, making him wish Sierra could hear the words. Seconds later, the rest of his comment sank in. The colonel had lumped the two of them together in their endeavors to help Sierra.

"All right, then, let's do this." Noah felt relieved. With the colonel on his side, he couldn't lose. And maybe, just maybe, Sierra would also get closer to her father. The real guy and not the military man.

"I'll make a few calls and see what I can find out."

Noah hesitated before saying goodbye. "How's she doing, if you don't mind me asking?"

Silence filled the air just long enough to worry Noah.

"I don't mind you asking. She and I are working a few things out, but Sierra's not herself. I've been a little worried, as I wasn't sure it was all injury related. My concern was perhaps PTSD, but now I'm wondering if it isn't heart related." The older man chuckled.

"Let's hope you're right. I'm assuming you've got my number from caller ID. Call me when you get a lead." Noah had no doubt the colonel could move mountains and they'd find Rhaegar. But it was his *heart related* comment that drove home the hardest. Dare he hope Sierra missed him, too?

Noah's phone lit up two days later, the colonel's name popping on the screen. His adrenaline spiked. He was optimistic it would be good news. "Good morning, sir."

"Good morning. And please, call me Charles. I've been sirred enough to last me a lifetime."

"Yes, sir, *ummm*...Charles. What did you find out?" Noah was anxious to get to the point and didn't want to read too much into the first-name basis.

"You were right, of course. It took a few phone calls, but I got what you wanted. The guy you're looking for is David Wainwright. He's been up in Alaska and without the internet or a phone. I had him tracked down and sent word to where he was staying. He's on his way back to where he lives in Maine with the dog now. I'll email you the address. He's been apprised of the situation and is expecting you. If you leave soon, you should have Rhaegar back in no time at all." This was great news, and he could hear the satisfaction in the colonel's voice.

"How's the dog? It will break Sierra's heart if anything's wrong." He'd often wondered about Rhaegar's condition.

"I like that you're concerned, but there's nothing to worry about. Dog's fine, but it sounds like he might be missing her as much as she's missing him."

Noah breathed a sigh of relief. "That's good news for sure. Thanks for doing this, sir. *Ummm*...Charles," he corrected. Calling him by his first name would take some getting used to.

"The thanks go to you for calling me to help. You did good, son. I'm sure Sierra will appreciate your effort." There was that word again. *Son.* The kind of word that made one feel good. Proud.

"Our efforts. Although most of the credit goes to you." Noah wasn't about to take anything from the man who'd made it all happen.

"Let's just hope you're right and she forgives us both."

"Amen to that." Noah hung up, eager to make a call and set up a meeting with David. If he left right after Kaylee got home from school, they'd be back late tonight, giving him two days to get everything else planned for the jubilee.

And Rhaegar and Sierra's reunion.

There was always a chance she wouldn't show up, but he was confident she would. Her promises were golden, and she wouldn't hurt Kaylee. And even if she didn't show up, it wouldn't change anything other than require him to make a trip to Boston with his special delivery.

Chapter Nineteen

♥

AFTER TALKING TO THE colonel—or as she tried to think of him now—her father, Sierra spent more time going over her time with the Jackson family. Mainly about Noah and how much she missed him.

Truth be told, she was glad she'd promised to go to the Veteran's Day Jubilee because it gave her an excuse to see Kaylee *and* Noah. Sierra had left more hurt than angry, but time had a way of smoothing over hurts. So did the new relationship with her father. It was still awkward, but at least they were both trying. Her mother, on the other hand, couldn't be more thrilled. Although, Sierra could do without her excessive mothering when it came to dealing with her daughter's injuries.

Sierra gazed out the window, sipping on her coffee. It occurred to her, that perhaps the answers she sought about what had happened in Afghanistan, were close at hand. Answers in the form of an expert strategic military man. *The colonel.* That she was even considering talking to him about what happened out in the field on a mission was a huge indicator of the improvement in their relationship.

Know no fear. Her own words drifted into her head. Words she'd used to encourage other soldiers. Words she needed to apply to her own life. Decision made, she took a deep breath and headed down the hall to her father's office. Sierra leaned in slightly and stuck her head past the door. "Got a minute?" she asked.

"Sure thing. Come in." He pointed to the seat across from his desk. His quick affirmative response was quite different from the last time she'd tried to get an audience with him.

"I think I'll stand if you don't mind."

"Okay. What's on your mind?" He closed a file on his desk and leaned back in his leather chair, his gaze never leaving her.

"Afghanistan. More specifically, what happened. I'd like your viewpoint as a military officer on what I'm about to tell you. I'm not looking for a sugar-coated opinion for my benefit."

He nodded. "I don't do sugar-coated, you of all people should know that."

"I do, but given the oddity of things between us lately…" Their relationship was changing, and she wasn't sure what to expect anymore. But she needed the cold, hard honesty the colonel would have given her not too long ago—before the wall between them had come tumbling down.

Her father smiled, the wrinkles on his face deepening. "Changes nothing when it comes to answers and truth. Fire away."

Sierra turned and gazed out the window, digging deep for confidence. She closed her eyes and began to tell the story as she remembered. It made it easier to think of her father as her commanding officer that she was giving a full report to. Sierra repeated every detail, including her doubts.

To his credit, the colonel remained silent through it all. When she finished, she opened her eyes and turned back to face him. His expression gave nothing away.

The colonel let out a deep breath and laced his fingers together on the desk, his gaze intent on her. "That was a tough place to be—for anyone. I'm sorry you had to go through it." It was as though another brick had fallen from the wall, the weariness in his eyes and shoulders a testament to his words.

"It's my fault, though, isn't it? I missed something, or I should've slowed down or should have... I don't know... done something differently." She wrung her hands together in front of her, fighting back the anguish as the memories assailed her.

"Sierra, it sounds like you had a fifty-fifty shot and lost. It happens. You had to make a split-second decision with no way of knowing the outcome. A soldier is trained to make the best decision given what information they have. Knowing you, you made the best decision." His words shocked her to the core.

She'd asked him not to patronize her, and that's what it sounded like he was doing. "But you don't know that." She couldn't keep the disappointment out of her voice.

The colonel sat back in his chair and shook his head. "Neither do you. What if the other trail was worse? There's no way to know what could have been different. From what I hear, you were brave and that you were responsible for saving many lives once Rhaegar picked up the scent. You need to cut yourself some slack and focus on the positives." Coming from the colonel, *cut yourself some slack* didn't jive. He didn't believe in cutting slack. To anyone.

"But not everyone was saved," she said, finally addressing the room's ticking bomb.

The colonel nodded. "True. But what about all the other soldiers who have fought and died for our country? Are their leaders responsible for their deaths? Does that ultimately make the commanders responsible since they're over all of the leaders? Where does the blame stop in a situation like this? Or do we acknowledge the truth? The guys who made and set the IED are at fault. It's the people we're fighting against who are at fault when you look at the big picture. We fight to protect the people of our country and our rights, and we fight to help other nations from being subjugated to acts of terror. If you let this destroy you, you're not honoring the memory of the fallen soldier—a man who believed in the cause."

It wasn't anything she hadn't heard before, but coming from the colonel, the words were like a jackhammer opening her heart for inspection. "I hear what you're saying, but I can't get it out of my head. The images keep haunting me and making me doubt myself." At the Jackson ranch, her nightmares had decreased, but since being home, they'd multiplied. A good night's sleep was hard to come by.

"You wouldn't be a good leader if they didn't. But you also wouldn't be a good leader if you let them hold you back from moving forward, whether in the military or life in general. Sierra don't let the past control you. Don't let the bad guys win."

"What do I do? How did you manage it?" She wasn't naïve enough to believe he'd gotten as far as he had without suffering losses within his troops.

He clasped his hands together like a steeple beneath his chin as if considering his answer. "Every person has their own way of coping. For me, it was to visit the families of the fallen soldiers under my command."

That was news to her, and more proof her father was not at all the man she'd once believed him to be. "I didn't know that."

"Well, it wasn't something I discussed at home. I tried to keep military life separate from home life, although it didn't always work. But it wasn't for the lack of trying, trust me."

It was the same thing she'd thought of doing. The apple didn't fall far from the tree. "I've thought about visiting Mrs. Brady, but I've been avoiding it. I'm not sure of the reception I'll get." *More like afraid.*

"Then visit her. You won't know until you try, and the daughter I know you to be, doesn't back down from anything," the colonel said, his voice vibrating with pride.

"Thank you." The compliment rang in her heart long after she left his office and all the way during the three-hour drive to Mrs. Brady's home. There was no sense putting it off, and she'd taken courage in her father's words and done exactly as he suggested.

Mrs. Brady had turned out to be a complete surprise. The woman was gracious, kind, and welcoming. They'd talked for hours, her words a healing balm to Sierra's soul. She didn't hold any grudges and had told Sierra the same thing everyone had been telling her. Being in the military was a choice, and although no one wanted to die, everyone knew it was always a possibility. It was their choice to take the risk.

Where the colonel had jackhammered her heart open, it was Mrs. Brady's words that filled the hole until it was overflowing. Robert Brady had died serving his country, a tragic loss, but he was an honorable man whose exemplary service was something his family could be proud of. Their son was a hero. Forever loved.

With a lighter heart, Sierra headed home. This time, her thoughts on Noah. Missing him was one thing. What to do about it was another.

Sierra was going to the jubilee, which included the ball, that much was for sure. She didn't want to miss out on life. On joy. On anything. *She'd found peace.*

Starting with her job, no matter what form it took. Her father had helped her understand that all the parts of a well-oiled machine were important, and the military consisted of many parts. It was up to her to figure out another position that would make her happy based on any limitations the military put her under after her return.

Secondly, with herself, and who she was as a person. She cared about Noah and was done running away from him, not that she knew what to do about her feelings. For that, she needed to know where Noah landed on the subject. But one thing was for sure, she wanted Noah in her life. She would take strength in whatever he was willing to share with her going forward. No commitments. Just friends. She wouldn't make promises she couldn't keep, but friendship—now that was a promise she could keep.

Nearing home, an idea hit her. Noah would be attending the ball and it was the perfect opportunity to prove to him she'd changed. For her secret prince, she wanted to take a huge leap of faith forward.

Correction. Sierra wanted to do this for herself. *Noah would be the bonus.*

It would be a chance to expose all her insecurities, proving that she was comfortable in her own skin. As for Noah, she wanted more than anything to see a light in his eyes as he gazed down at her. She wanted to dance with him. As friends, of course. But it would be something to keep her warm on a dark night when she deployed again.

There wasn't much time to prepare, but if she used the single-minded determination she applied to everything else in her life, she could make it happen.

Cinderella was going to a ball.

Chapter Twenty

♥

"I DON'T SEE HER anywhere, Daddy. What if she doesn't come?" Kaylee asked Noah for the tenth time in the past fifteen minutes. "Are you sure grandma told her only the races were canceled today and not the ball?" They had to arrive earlier than most to get Rhaegar settled in where he wouldn't upset the Veteran's Day Jubilee or ruin the surprise.

Noah had planned this moment down to the very last detail, except the part where it rained, and the goat races were canceled. At least his mother had reassured him Sierra's response text said she was still coming to the ball and that she hadn't wanted to disappoint Kaylee on an already disappointing day.

Sierra always had Kaylee's best interest at heart. However, the result of the rain meant presenting Rhaegar would come with the added difficulty of arranging the meeting at the ball. Noah had the same worry as his daughter, not that he'd share that information.

The colonel had also reassured him Sierra was coming, not to mention, he and his wife would be in attendance. It was all part of the surprise for Sierra.

Kaylee had been a blessing the past forty-eight hours—her help with Rhaegar proof she was ready for a dog of her own. He had a feeling his daughter was as in love with Rhaegar, as Noah was with Sierra. Kaylee was over the moon with excitement to see Sierra tonight and show her their surprise.

He went out on the balcony again to check on the dog. "Hey, boy. I'm sure she's coming. We just need a little faith." Telling the dog that seemed to be more for Noah's benefit, and the dog rubbed up against his hand searching for a good petting. "I promise I'll bring Sierra to you straight away."

Woof. Woof.

Noah laughed and headed back inside. Rhaegar was smart, healthy, and determined—just like Sierra. The thought made him smile. He spotted the colonel with a woman on the side of the room talking to some uniformed soldiers. Sierra's mother—judging by the way she stayed close to the colonel.

Noah scanned the room, and a movement at the door caught his attention.

Sierra.

She was more beautiful than he could have imagined. The sea-green chiffon gown fit her body like a glove, revealing every inch of her athletic curves. Her hair was styled with ringlets and piled high on her head, exposing her throat's graceful lines. As much as he loved his country girl in jeans, one word came to mind seeing her in this dress. *Stunning.*

The significance of Sierra showing up in a gown and not her military uniform wasn't lost on Noah. How it came about was another matter. Later, he'd have to ask, but right now, he didn't care. She'd caught sight of him and was headed his way, her gaze never wavering as she approached. Her shy smile gave him hope he still had a chance with her.

Kaylee ran up to him and pointed in Sierra's direction. "Daddy, she's here. She's so beautiful. Like

Cinderella." The adoration and excitement in his daughter's voice echoed his own sentiment. "I can't wait to show her the surprise."

"But remember, not a word. You know the plan." Noah wasn't sure Kaylee could pull this part off. A seven-year-old keeping a colossal surprise was like the sun trying to stop shining.

"Yes, Daddy. Just hurry it up." Kaylee laughed, pulling him toward Sierra.

He reached for Sierra's hand. "Cinderella," he whispered, his voice dropping to a husky tone of appreciation, and using the name Kaylee had planted in his head. "I'm so pleased you came to the ball."

"It's nice to see you both. Of course, I came. A promise—"

"Is a promise," Kaylee finished for her. "I was worried because they canceled the goat races, but Daddy kept telling me not to worry."

"I'm sorry about the races, honey. I know you had your heart set on beating Tommy, but God knows best, and there's a reason he didn't want you to race. Sometimes, you have to trust in the greater good."

"I was upset, but not anymore. Tommy's just a boy, and some things are just so much more important. It's a good thing you came because we've got—"

"Kaylee, remember what we talked about. Sierra just got here. Perhaps you could get her a glass of punch so I can talk to her for a minute," Noah said, using his don't-argue-with-me voice to help keep her focused.

Kaylee looked up at him, hands on her hips. "Yes, Daddy. But hurry. A girl shouldn't have to wait forever." She turned with a flounce and walked away.

"What was that all about?" Sierra asked, her gaze following Kaylee's departure.

"Nothing. She's happy to see you is all."

"Okay, if you say so. I missed her, too." Sierra seemed different. Happier. And it was more than the dress. There was a glow about her that hadn't been there before, as though she'd made peace with the world.

"I hope you missed more than my daughter." Noah pulled her close, lowering his voice for privacy. "I'm sorry for the way I ran you off and hope you'll forgive me. I think I was running scared. About us. But I'm not now." He was hoping to clear the air between them, prepping the way for the big reveal.

"I'm sorry, too. I know it wasn't easy dealing with my difficulties, and honestly, I get it about Kaylee. I've come to realize that kind of protective streak comes with loving someone. I needed time to figure out who I am and to stop taking my anger and frustrations out on everyone around me. I've still got a lot of adjusting to do, but I'm trying." It sounded as though she'd come a long way while she was gone. Further than he could've hoped. Did that also mean there might be hope for the two of them?

"So, I see." He grinned, letting his gaze drift down to her feet, and slowly travel back up, taking in each inch of perfection, and stopping on her face. Noah couldn't believe what Sierra was saying. "Will Cinderella save me a place on her dance card later? Maybe two or three?"

"Why not now?" She gestured to the dance floor where several couples danced.

"Tempting, but no. I've got a surprise for you first. And after, I'll claim my first dance and a kiss as my reward," he said, his grin growing wider if it were possible. His bold declaration caught Sierra by surprise.

"A reward kiss for a dance?" she countered; one eyebrow arched slightly as she gazed up at him. "You think highly of your dance skills, Mr. Noah Jackson." He'd missed her and her humor, but he wouldn't have to miss her anymore, not if he had anything to say about it. "No. A kiss as a reward for your surprise."

"Still bold. I'm here for Kaylee, remember," she said, her grin causing the dimples at each side of her mouth to deepen.

"Dressed like you are? I hardly think that's for Kaylee. I'd much prefer to think it's for my benefit." He pulled her closer, daring her to disagree. Only a hint of space separated them.

"Maybe I'm dressed this way for me. You can believe what you want, but I'm not promising a kiss. Only that we will go back to being friends." Not exactly what he had in mind, but now that she was here, he had all night to convince her more than friends was a better idea.

"Trust me on this, your surprise will be so good, you'll want to kiss me for a week." He winked.

Sierra shook her head and laughed. "But I'm only here for the night," she teased, fanning her face with an imaginary fan.

"Plans change."

Kaylee came up and handed Sierra a glass of punch that matched the blush in her cheeks. "Can we do the surprise now, Daddy. Please?"

"Yes, we can go now," he said, giving the green light.

"Yay!" Kaylee exclaimed as she raced ahead toward the balcony.

Sierra started to follow. "I'm really curious now. I can't imagine what you two are up to."

"You're probably right about that." Noah laughed and took her by the hand. "Trust me, Cinderella?"

"I do." Her answer had his heart racing like he hadn't known was possible. And for the first time in a long time, he started thinking about those two little words and the immense possibilities surrounding them.

Chapter Twenty-One

♥

SIERRA DIDN'T HAVE A clue what the two of them were up to, but she quickly caught the fever of excitement and knew whatever it was, it had to be good. When she'd walked into the ballroom, she had zeroed in on Noah at once. Through the sea of people beautifully dressed in gowns of every color, men in tuxedos, and soldiers in military uniform, it was as though there was a neon sign above Noah's head saying *here I am.*

And when he'd spotted her, the look in his eyes had given her the confidence to move forward. As if floating through the air, she'd crossed the room in high heels like a pro, not once faltering. Falling flat on her face would have ruined the moment for sure.

Now, as he led her out of the ballroom and down the hall, her arm firmly tucked under his, her confidence soared higher. She'd never seen Noah dressed in a tuxedo, and he was a dashing man, looking every inch her Prince Charming for the evening. She was used to him in hospital scrubs and jeans, but this look was the stuff of fairy tales and young girl's dreams.

"You're gonna love this," Kaylee exclaimed when they stopped in front of a set of double glass doors, the view outside blocked by elegant lacy curtains.

"Then lead on, and don't keep me in suspense." Sierra took a step toward the door, unable to quell the rising excitement in her chest.

"Wait. One word of caution," Noah said, not letting go of her arm.

Caution. That was not a word Sierra associated with a pleasant surprise. "Okay," she said tentatively, pausing to look up at him.

"I hadn't calculated on your dress or heels. And as gorgeous as you look, I think you should lose the shoes. And I'm praying your dress survives because I'd hate to see it ruined."

Now Noah had really lost her. "Doesn't sound like a very nice surprise," she said, leaning down to remove her spiked heels.

"Oh, it is. You'll see," Noah said, holding out his hand.

Sierra handed them over, more than a little curious and nervous about what to expect on the other side of the door. Kaylee's excitement was the one thing that kept her moving forward. And of course, she trusted Noah.

"Go ahead, Kaylee," Noah said, his voice light, adding to the moment's suspense.

"It's about time." The little girl reached for the door and pushed it wide open.

At first glance, Sierra didn't see anything, and Kaylee stepped back to let her pass by. As she stepped through the doorway, a movement off to the side caught her attention. A dog lay next to the railing, his head raised, his nose sniffing the air as he glanced in their direction.

It took Sierra a split second to understand what she was seeing.

"Rhaegar." The word slipped out of her mouth in a reverent hush. But it was enough for her faithful friend to hear loud and clear, and he bounded toward her. Sierra dropped to her knees, not caring about her dress. She pulled him close, wrapping her arms around his neck.

Tears filled her eyes and spilled over. Adrenaline raced through her body as the reality of the moment settled in. *Rhaegar was here.*

"Hey, boy. How are you? I've missed you so much."

Woof. Woof. Rhaegar licked her face, letting Sierra know he felt the same.

Noah had found Rhaegar. It made her like him all that much more. Love him if she was truthful with herself. Not that loving him changed anything. It would only make it more difficult when she left. She pushed away the thought, hugging Rhaegar and basking in the moment of their reunion.

He lifted his paw and placed it on her shoulder, as if to reassure himself she was real, followed by several more doggy licks.

Noah's comment about her dress and the heels came back to her, and Sierra finally understood the cryptic remarks—but the dress didn't matter. What mattered was Rhaegar, Noah, and Kaylee. Sierra looked up at Noah through a blur of tears. "Thank you both. I can't believe you found him. How did you manage to do this when I couldn't?"

"My pleasure, but honestly, I can't take most of the credit. I had about the same luck as you did. It was your father who came through and pulled a few strings to make it happen."

"My father? I don't understand."

"He's telling the truth." Her father's voice came from the doorway, and Sierra looked up, stunned he was even at the ball, much less responsible for finding Rhaegar. In full uniform, her father looked regal, more so than Sierra ever remember. There was something different about him. The love shining in his eyes for her, something she'd never noticed before. Her mother stood next to him in a ballgown of the finest silk, looking beautiful next to the colonel.

"I don't understand," Sierra said, trying to assimilate the information. And you're here...at the ball. You didn't say a word about coming when I told you I would be attending."

Her father smiled. "That's true, but I had my reasons." He moved closer and bent down to pet the dog. "Hey, Rhaegar. It's nice to finally meet you."

Sierra continued to pet Rhaegar, unwilling to let him go now that he was by her side. "What kind of reasons?" she asked her father, trying to unravel the mystery.

"For starters, when Noah called me for help, I realized it was the best way possible for both of us to show you how much we care. We've both made some mistakes we'd like you to forgive." Her dad continued to pet the dog as he talked, sharing in the moment with her.

"Done. How could I ever be upset with anyone who brought Rhaegar back to me?" A fresh wave of tears spilled over as she stood. She kept her hand connected with Rhaegar, unwilling to let go. She glanced at Noah and gave him a smile, letting him know she forgave him for everything.

"Thank you. In my case, it's more than I deserve, and I appreciate the second chance." Her father stood and held out his arms.

Without hesitation, Sierra stepped in close, accepting his hug, something she couldn't remember happening in the past. At least not like this. This was real.

"The other reason I'm here is because Commander Wilcox asked me to attend. He didn't know I was already planning to be here."

"Commander Wilcox is here?" she asked, stunned. Her commander hadn't said anything to her.

"Yes. He wants to present you with the Silver Star Medal and Staff Sergeant Rhaegar with the Lois Pope K-9 Medal of Courage. Turns out, they were looking for Rhaegar as well, hoping to present the medals to you both at the same time. It was unfortunate the man taking care of him had gone to Alaska and was out of communication, but it turns out it was for the best. Rhaegar has a clean bill of health."

Medals were for bravery. It would seem everyone saw her efforts in Afghanistan differently than she did, or than she dared to accept. "I can't believe this is happening," she said, letting the tears run down her face unchecked. She didn't care who saw or shared in this joyful moment. Sierra turned to Noah. "And you knew?"

"I did. Charles mentioned it after we located Rhaegar. My job was to keep him safe until the ball. His job was to make sure you didn't back out of coming." Noah stood there beaming, as if he'd just handed her the moon—because he had.

"Not a chance. A promise—"

"Is a promise," Kaylee exclaimed, moving in for a hug of her own. Something Sierra was happy to give. She'd missed her so much, and it had only been days.

"I brought your uniform, figuring you'd want to be in it for the ceremonial presentation," her father said. This came as a shock because she knew how he felt about her in the military. But now she knew why he felt the way he did, and she didn't hold it against him anymore.

"Do I have to wear it? What's the protocol?" she asked, much preferring to stay just as she was. The adoration in Noah's eyes was enough to make her throw protocol to the wind, if possible.

"Nothing that requires you wear it. You're not here in a military capacity, it's not a military-sponsored event, and you're on leave. So, it's your choice." The colonel's answer surprised her, but it was a welcome one.

"Good. I think I'll stay exactly as I am."

"You look beautiful, darling. I'm so proud of you," her mother said, moving in for a hug.

"I like exactly who you are, no matter what you're wearing," Noah said, moving to stand next to her.

"I agree." High praise from both of her favorite men. "The military is lucky to have you, and I don't think you being in a dress is going to stop them from recognizing that fact."

"Thanks, Colonel," Sierra said, unable to believe all the things her father was saying.

"It's Dad, not Colonel Winters to you. And that's an order."

"Yes, sir." She smiled. "I mean, *ummm*...yes, Dad," she corrected after noticing his scowl. Ever since they'd reconnected, she'd had a difficult time deciding how to address him. This made it easy. It was an order she could follow.

"Sorry I'm late to the big reveal, but I got held up in traffic," Tank said from the doorway as he stepped out onto the balcony, a beautiful brunette on his arm. Laura followed not far behind them, making their little party complete.

"You knew? And all the times I talked to you; you didn't give so much as a hint." She tried to sound put out but couldn't make happen. Happiness had a way of taking over everything.

"We all knew, dearie. But no one was about to ruin the surprise. You deserve tonight," Laura said, coming forward to hug her.

"Listen up, everyone," Tank spoke up, quieting the group. "I'd like to introduce you to Camilla, the friend from Boston I've been telling you about."

"It's nice to meet you all," Camilla said before glancing up at Tank, a questioning expression on her face.

"Girlfriend," Tank corrected, which explained her gaze.

"It's lovely to finally meet you, too. We were beginning to wonder if you were real." Sierra laughed, moving forward to hug the woman. She was so proud of Tank for taking the next step. It was proof he was well on the road to recovery.

"Oh, I'm real. This lug head was just slow to come around and admitting he cared," Camilla teased.

"Interesting. Considering I've known for months he left the military to be with you," Sierra shot back with a grin.

Tank, on the other hand, didn't seem to care for her admission of truth.

"Hey, I always told you I'd get you back for the pip-squeak comment. Guess we're even." Sierra laughed.

"Reckon so," Tank said, taking Camilla's hand, and signaling them as a couple.

They all went back into the ballroom, her father searching out the commander. The two of them headed toward the stage.

Sierra still couldn't believe this was happening. Rhaegar deserved this medal, of that there was no doubt. But it was hard to accept an award for herself when she'd done what any other soldier would have done—saved as many lives as possible.

Commander Wilcox gave a speech, most of which Sierra didn't hear. The tale of what happened was one she knew far too well. The sound of clapping brought her out of the memory, and people made way for her and Staff Sergeant Rhaegar to take the stage.

The commander placed the medals around their necks, shaking hands. And paws.

"Congratulations, Sergeant Winters. You showed exemplary service to your country, and I couldn't be prouder to have you on my team." His words were high praise, and she reveled in the moment.

It was true. No one blamed her for what went wrong, and they believed she was responsible for what had gone right. It was truly a moment she'd never forget. "Thank you, sir. On both of our behalves."

Woof. Woof. The crowd burst into another round of applause and laughter.

Sierra spotted Noah and her parents toward the front left side of the room. Her father beamed as he accepted several handshakes from some of his friends. Her dad was proud of her. As if knowing she was thinking of him, he gazed up at her and touched his heart.

Any tears she'd valiantly fought off, fell like rain.

The rest of the evening passed by in a blur, no matter how hard she tried to slow things down. Cinderella's midnight was fast approaching, and she'd have to leave. But it was a night she'd never forget.

"See you December 6th, Winters," Commander Wilcox said as he readied to leave the event. Sierra still couldn't believe he'd driven up to personally oversee the ceremony. "And congratulations."

"Yes, sir. And with any luck, the docs will clear me to return to full duty. At first, I wasn't following the doctor's orders the way I should have been, but lately, I've been on point, and I can finally tell the difference in the healing." Except, the thought of returning brought her no joy. It was all she'd ever know, but things had changed.

If she deployed, she'd be leaving Noah and Kaylee behind, not to mention Rhaegar. It's not like she could take him with her overseas. For the first time, the thought of what she'd leave behind was a concern. It was one thing when she didn't have Rhaegar by her side, but now that he was back in her life, her decisions would be affected.

And then there was that kiss after the pizza party at Noah's new house. She hadn't been able to get it out of her head. She also couldn't help thinking about the thank you kiss Noah was expecting tonight.

"I think it's time for me to have one last dance before Cinderella disappears," Noah whispered in her ear, sending shivers down her spine. They'd danced several dances already, but he'd graciously allowed many soldiers eager for a dance to whisk her around the ballroom floor. Not that he hadn't watched with a protective, jealous expression permanently etched on his face the whole time.

Sierra slid into his arms willingly, savoring the moment. Her last dance. "Wonderful idea, Prince Noah," she teased. Strong arms enfolded her as they danced to the dreamy strains of a waltz. Rhaegar and Kaylee sat at a table on the sidelines, watching with interest.

It was obvious the two of them had become attached, and the timing of Noah's decision to give in to Kaylee's request for a dog had become much shorter. Returning her focus to her handsome prince, she floated around the dance floor under his excellent guidance. The man was a master dancer, which was lucky for her because it covered her inabilities. It all came down to trusting him, which she did. Explicitly.

"You don't have to leave," Noah said, his voice low and husky. "You said yourself your contract is ending. Or if you reenlist, make this your home base. Kaylee wants you to stay. She missed you. I missed you and want you to stay." Noah was laying all the cards on the table. She didn't want to have this conversation now.

"I can't stay. My life is the military, and that's not going to change anytime soon. You know that." This was the part where Cinderella lost her slipper and disappeared into the night. The unwanted truth lay between them like the Grand Canyon. "I can't promise I'll come home. It's a promise I might not be able to keep."

"But it's also not fair to put us on hold."

"I'm not asking you to wait," she said, forcing out the words that would put an end to what was blossoming between them.

"That's because you don't trust that I can handle whatever life delivers. Good and bad. I prefer to take it all as a package deal, letting the ups offset life's downs. There are never guarantees about anything, but one has to be willing to try." They would never agree on this because Noah had never seen the destruction up close. Not the way she had.

"Maybe not, but it's the way it has to be." Sierra could feel Noah pulling away and shutting down emotionally.

He executed the moves perfectly, but he'd fallen silent after her declaration. It was as though the magic of the night had worn off. There'd be no kiss. The music ended, and with it, Sierra's courage. If she didn't leave now, she'd have a tough go of it later.

"I'm sorry," she said, slipping out of his arms and making her way toward the sidelines where Rhaegar and Kaylee waited.

She leaned down to give Kaylee a hug, relieved Noah hadn't followed her. It would only make things harder. "Bye, sweetheart. I've got to head home now. Thank you so much for a wonderful evening and the best surprise ever."

"I knew you'd like it." Kaylee beamed. "When will I see you again?"

"I don't know. I've got to report back to the base, and it depends on my schedule." Sierra brushed back a lock of hair from Kaylee's face.

"Okay. Just don't forget us. Bye, Miss Sierra. Bye, Rhaegar." Kaylee pulled the dog in for a hug.

"I won't." Sierra took Rhaegar's leash and led him away, but not before glancing over to where Noah stood watching from the sidelines, a look of devastation on his face.

She forced herself to the other side of the room where her parents stood talking to a friend. Sierra resolved not to look back again. She couldn't, or her resolve might waiver.

The military was her life, and that was just the way things had to be. And she'd never promise to come home when she couldn't guarantee it. Too many people stood to be hurt if she was selfish and gave in to what she wanted—which was Noah.

And love.

Chapter Twenty-Two

♥

NOAH HAD DRIVEN HOME last night in a blue mood, much the same as Kaylee. His daughter wasn't at all pleased with Sierra's departure, given there was no see-you-soon date in place. There was still some time left before she had to report back to the base, but instead of saying they could spend it together, Sierra had shut him out cold.

He'd held out great hope everything would work out. And it had for Sierra and her father, but she obviously didn't have strong enough feelings for Noah. He was tempted to call her this morning, but she'd made her position clear. He also had Kaylee to think about. She wasn't old enough to understand, and he hated that she was left to deal with another woman's departure from her life.

All along, he'd told himself getting close to Sierra wasn't a promising idea. After he'd let his guard down, he'd proven himself right. Next time, he'd listen to his gut. Heck, there wouldn't be a next time. And if there was... No, that kind of thinking would lead him straight to Boston to convince Sierra to change her mind.

Something he wouldn't do. Couldn't do. Staying and giving them a chance had to be her choice. It wasn't like she didn't know where he stood on the matter. His declaration couldn't have been any more to the point. His mother would think he'd bungled his apology, but Noah knew it wasn't the case. This was all about Sierra now.

She'd admitted she cared and that she was trying to move forward. But that's not what Noah saw. What he saw was someone running scared. And the only person who could fix that was Sierra.

Three weeks went by and Sierra was no closer to getting over Noah than when she left the jubilee. It didn't help that her father grilled her about what happened, or that her mother tried to convince her to reconsider. Her father's respect for Noah was just one more point in the Mr. Amazing category. Winning over her father was no small matter.

Thanksgiving Day had been the hardest. Blessings and giving thanks for what one had in life always led her thoughts back to Noah and Kaylee. Her one consolation through the days and weeks was Rhaegar. But now, even her trusted canine was a reminder of Noah.

Rhaegar was the best therapy Sierra could have. Together, they ran and worked out like old times. Each day, her leg grew stronger, and she could tell she was making huge leaps of progress. Enough that she'd even ditched the cane full time. Not to mention, sleeping each night came easier.

At least it did when thoughts of Noah didn't keep her awake.

Sierra wasn't due back to the base until the 6th, but she decided to return a few days early. Nothing keeping her in Boston with her parents. Although she enjoyed spending quality time with them, they were still her parents. She'd long ago found her freedom, and it was a hard thing to give up for too long. She finished packing her bags and loaded the car, ready to head for home. Her home.

With Rhaegar by her side, she went to find her father. "I'm leaving, Dad," she said, poking her head into his office.

"Are you sure you're doing the right thing, honey?" he asked, setting down his pen as he stood.

"Honestly, no. But it's the best thing. Remember the weighing-choices and making-best-decision spiel you gave me? That's what I'm doing. The military is my life." Who was she trying to prove it to? Herself or her dad? Because this felt more like she was trying to prove to herself she was justified in leaving without saying a word to Noah. All without opening the door she'd firmly closed out of fear of hurting Noah and Kaylee, worse than her leaving now would hurt them.

"It's a choice. But what about Noah? I know you care about each other. I managed to have a good relationship with your mother while I was in the military. Lots of people have successful relationships while serving their country. They're a team." Up until recently, she'd believed it hadn't been right for her mother. It was hard to grasp that everything she'd believed growing up wasn't the truth. Harder still to change and do something about it.

He was right—just not for Sierra. "I get it. But the idea of getting injured or killed and letting my family down or hurting them keeps me from wanting to go that route. I've seen it up close and personal when things don't work out. It's not pretty." She had ten years of experience watching to be exact, and it was difficult to see every time it happened. People grieved and were hurt, their broken hearts leaving a trail of tears. There was no way she wanted to cause anyone that kind of pain.

"But those people have the choice of whether to be strong or not, whether to move on with their lives. In doing so, they honor a fallen warrior. Besides, I married your mother because I knew she was strong enough to manage anything."

"You're wrong. Mom's never been strong, but luckily, nothing ever happened to you." How could her father not know the truth after all these years and not see her mother as a weak woman who needed him?

"That's where you're mistaken. Something did happen once. And you'd be surprised what a tower of strength your mother was and has always been. I wouldn't have had a successful career in the military without her."

All understanding ceased. Her father was giving her mother credit for his career. None of it made sense. "What are you talking about?"

He crossed the room to stand next to her and took her hand. "All you ever saw was her missing me when I was gone because she loves me. And doting on me when I was home because she loves me. It was her way to make sure I knew it and never forgot. But there were letters and phone calls when I was away, that's where her real strength came shining through like the Northern Star calling me home. When I was injured and overseas, her words of encouragement kept me pushing harder to get better and come home to you both. Those were some dark days." His voice had gone low as if remembering the past brought up memories best left alone.

Her life had been a lie. Her *mother* had given her father strength. Not at all the picture Sierra had of her. "I don't remember you getting hurt."

"I was in the wrong place at the wrong time. We didn't want you to know. I tried so hard to shield you from everything. But, honey, it was the loving support of your mother that saw me through the toughest times. Noah's that kind of guy, too. But I've said enough. It's your life and decision, and I'll stand behind you one hundred percent no matter what you chose to do. I just want you to be happy." Her father pulled her close for a bear hug, something he did with greater frequency ever since the ball. It was as though the last remaining bricks of the wall between them had come down.

"I'll think about everything you said, I promise." And Sierra always kept her promises.

"I hope you'll be home for Christmas. Don't be a stranger in your own home anymore. We've missed having you around."

"I'll see what I can do. I love you, Dad." Sierra realized she meant every word. She did love him.

"I love you, too, sweetheart." He stepped back to let her go, his arms falling to his sides.

She turned and left, her steps a little slower as she went to find her mother. "I'm leaving, Mom," she said, finding her in the kitchen.

"I wish you didn't have to go back yet." Her mom wiped her flour-covered hands on her apron and came to hug Sierra.

"I'll try to be back in a few weeks for Christmas."

"Promise?" her mother asked.

"I can't promise because I don't know what my schedule will look like, but I will let you know as soon as I do."

"Thank you, sweetheart. It's been great having you home and seeing you and your father grow close. It's like a wish come true for me," she said, tears glistening in her eyes.

"It is good. I love you, Mom."

"Love you, too, sweetheart. It's a good thing you still have your old living quarters, or you'd be stuck having to find a hotel with Rhaegar."

"I know. And I'm still not sure what to do now because if I stay with what I'm doing it would mean getting another dog. Lots of decisions to be made, but you can be sure they will include Rhaegar now that I have him back in my life."

"Call me when you get to the base and get settled in. Keep me posted."

"Will do." She led Rhaegar to the car and threw her pack into the backseat, letting the dog ride up front with her.

Two hours down the road and two hours of conversation later, Rhaegar closed his eyes. She'd talked his ear off like she always did. That's what friends were for, and Rhaegar was the best listener ever.

If only he could answer.

There was only one thing Sierra knew for certain. Leaving felt wrong. *Instinct.* Just like when she'd picked between the two trails. She'd been wrong then. *How do you know the other trail wasn't worse?* Her father's words echoed in her head. She didn't. And therein lay the problem because there was no way of ever knowing. Just like with Noah. He was the other path now, and she'd never know if she didn't pause long enough to find out. *Take a chance.*

Sierra should feel some level of satisfaction. She was returning to the base, her military career, and hopefully, active duty if the doc on base cleared her mentally and physically. In what role the clearance would bring would work itself out over the next few weeks. But instead of feeling like she was making a huge step back to normal, it felt like she was running away.

Something she'd never done in her life.

The more she thought about it, the more she recognized the truth. Her heart confirmed it. She was running away from Noah and a relationship and future with him because she was afraid of getting hurt. Yes, there was a huge concern over the pain she'd put them through if anything happened to her, but Noah was clearly willing to take the chance.

He was brave, and she was a coward. Not a word she liked applied to herself. Not one bit. *Never be afraid of anything*. Her personal motto had been destroyed in the blink of an eye.

She loved the military, but she loved Noah more. For the first time in her life, she considered a life outside of the military. She didn't want one or the other—she wanted it all. Only *all* had taken on a new meaning. All meant life with Noah and Kaylee, the military, and even the job with the *GiddyUp Kids* program Chad had offered her.

The closer she got to the base, the more solid her plan of action became. By the time she cleared the security gate, she had it all worked out. Sierra wanted it all, and therefore, she'd settle for nothing less.

Chapter Twenty-Three

♥

WITH ONLY A FEW days to Christmas, Noah had kept busy. Between his mother, Bruce, and Kaylee, they'd managed to get everything moved into the new house. Not a day went by that he didn't think of Sierra and wonder what she was doing. She would have already reported back to duty and had moved on with her life without so much as a backward glance.

The void in his heart hadn't healed, and it only got worse the closer they got to Christmas. His mother had pulled out all stops and managed to get the place decorated, but it reminded him of the conversation he'd had with Sierra while standing in his living room.

There were chairs in front of the glass window overlooking the valley. A place to watch the wildlife, and where one got a sense of peace from the view as it stretched out as far as the eye could see. Snow blanketed the ground in thick waves, the moonlight shimmering off the surface. She'd called it magical.

He'd bought the chairs and a little table to go in between but so far hadn't used them. It *was* a magical place for two, and without Sierra, the magic wasn't the same. Kaylee preferred the couch and sitting around the newly decorated tree, so it really hadn't mattered. Even after a month, his daughter hadn't stopped talking about Sierra and Rhaegar or pleading with him to call her and ask her to visit.

Noah was tempted. Truly tempted.

Kaylee ran into the room. "Look, Daddy. I made Miss Sierra a Christmas ornament in case she shows up. And I made a wish upon a star. And, and..." She broke off, her voice going soft.

"What's wrong, honey?" he asked.

"She's not coming, is she? It wasn't like she promised." His daughter's lower lip trembled as she fought to deal with emotions welling up inside her.

"No, honey, she's not. But we will have a smashing Christmas. Grandma and Uncle Bruce and Camilla are coming over to celebrate in the new house with us." He was doing his best to cheer her up. "I think you should hang the decoration up anyway. That way, it's as if Sierra's here with us."

"That's a great idea, Daddy." Kaylee went and reached up on her tippy toes to hang the ornament as high as she could. "I miss her."

"I do, too, pumpkin. I do, too."

Lights flashed across the room, drawing his attention to a new arrival pulling up the driveway. His mother planned to stop by and drop off some food for Christmas dinner, but she was early. "Grandma's here," he called out to Kaylee, knowing it would cheer her up.

"Yippee." She ran ahead of Noah and pulled open the door. Except it wasn't his mother who stood there.

"Sierra," Kaylee squealed. "You came. And Rhaegar." She ran out the door to hug both new arrivals. Noah felt like doing the same but held back, partly stunned, and partly cautious, his heart still aching for the woman who stood on the doorstep.

"Hiya, munchkin. Surprise." Sierra was talking to Kaylee but looking directly at him. "Hope it's okay that I'm here." Her eyes sparkled with hope, and the vibrant joy radiating from her presence was enough to fill him with a peace he hadn't known since she left.

"Of course, silly. I wished upon a star for you to come, and here you are." Kaylee pulled Sierra by the hand into the house. "I have so much to tell you."

Noah laughed at his daughter's enthusiasm. "Kaylee's right, you are welcome. How'd you know we moved into the new house? Or did you stop by the ranch first?"

She shook her head and grinned. "Tank clued me in."

"My brother? He didn't say anything about you coming." Bruce had known and could've put him out of his misery, but he'd remained silent. Not something Noah would let slide when he saw him later today.

"He is my friend. Who else would I ask?" Sierra said, as if it should have been obvious.

"Call me, perhaps?" They were friends, or at least they had been. He hoped they still were.

"And ruin the surprise? Not on your life. Call it payback for the massive surprise you pulled on me." Sierra laughed.

"Let me take your coat." He reached out to pet Rhaegar while waiting for Sierra to shrug out of it. Her cheeks were flushed a pretty pink and given she hadn't been out of the car for long, he wanted to think it was because of his presence.

"Thank you," she said, handing him the jacket and pausing as if unsure what to do next.

"Come see the tree." Kaylee's eyes were big and round as she pulled her into the living room. Leave it to his daughter to break the ice.

"How beautiful," Sierra exclaimed, moving around to view it from every angle and reaching out to touch some of the decorations. "Where did you get so many unique ornaments? This is your first Christmas here."

"But not my first Christmas, silly. We get special decorations every year and keep them to hang the next year and the next. I helped pick out the tree and decorate it," Kaylee explained.

"What a great idea, and you did a wonderful job. I think it's the prettiest tree in Hallbrook. Your daddy's lucky to have a special helper like you." Sierra's words were like magic dust to Kaylee.

"Did you hear that, Daddy? She thinks it's the prettiest one in town. I think so, too."

Noah chuckled. "I agree, sweetheart. Why don't you take Rhaegar and show him your new room?" he suggested. His daughter wouldn't let him get a word in edgewise if he didn't give her something to do.

"But I want to show Miss Sierra my new room," she said, a frown forming on her face. "Are you gonna stay the night? I got bunk beds, and you can stay with me. Daddy said it's for when friends want to spend the night, and you're a friend. Right, Miss Sierra?"

"Absolutely. Best friends forever." Sierra held up her pinky. "Pinky promise."

"Yes!" Kaylee exclaimed, holding up her own pinky and joining forces with her friend.

"Now that we have that established, perhaps you'll do as I ask and let me and Miss Sierra chat a minute. I haven't seen her a while, and we need to catch up. I promise I'll bring her to your room as soon as possible."

Kaylee looked back and forth between them, a sudden light in her eyes. "I get it. You want to *talk*

talk to her. Like the time you kissed her. That sounds like the best idea ever. Come on, Rhaegar. Let's leave them alone." His daughter giggled as she left the room, the dog following her.

"I'm sorry. She gets her mind on something, and it's like a freight train coming through." Noah wasn't sure what else to say by way of apology. A kiss sounded like a pretty fantastic idea to him also, but first, he had to know why she was here.

"It's okay. I like Kaylee's enthusiasm." Sierra grinned.

He couldn't put off asking any longer. "So, umm, why are you here? Don't get me wrong, I'm happy to see you. But after the way things ended, I can't help but be cautious." Who was he kidding? He wanted to throw caution to the wind and haul her into his arms for the kiss he'd been denied the night of the ball and every night since then.

"I'm here for you. And Kaylee." He'd never seen such a beautiful and confident smile in all his life. "And for this." She stepped closer, wrapping her arms around his neck. "I've been waiting weeks for another one of these." Sierra pulled his head lower and kissed him. A toe-curling, knock-your-socks off, magical kiss.

"Then I'm glad you showed up because I've needed the same thing." He grinned, pulling her into his arms. He still wasn't sure what had changed, but this was the best Christmas present ever.

"That was quite the kiss, Mr. Jackson. Worth waiting for." Sierra leaned her forehead against his, her smile radiant.

"Glad to be of service, Sergeant Winters."

"About that. It's Sierra. Just Sierra." Her grin grew wider if it were possible, but it was her fingers running through his hair and her words that held him spellbound.

"There's nothing *just* about you, but I don't understand." Seconds later, the realization hit him, and shock rippled through every inch of his body.

She could only mean one thing. "Oh, I get it, I think." He hoped.

"Bingo." She laughed, pulling him in for another quick kiss.

"I think I do anyway. How long are you staying?"

"That depends on you," she said, stepping back out of his arms, her voice growing serious.

"What do you mean?"

"It's not a quick answer. Pour us a glass of wine, and I'll tell you a story. I noticed the chairs you bought. A magical place, was I right?"

"I wouldn't know. I haven't sat there yet. I think I was waiting for you to share the magic."

Her smile was proof he'd been right to wait. "Sounds perfect. Wine, and then we talk."

Noah opened a bottle, poured two glasses, and carried them over to where Sierra sat gazing out at the moonlit view.

"It's even more beautiful than I imagined."

"I quite agree," he said, but Noah was busy looking at Sierra as he sat in the chair next to her.

"I'm not sure where to start, but here goes. After I left here, I was brokenhearted, but it was of my own doing. You must believe me when I say I didn't want to. But all I've ever known is the military life, and I couldn't picture being the woman who went off to war while her hubby stays home and manages the kids. I worried about what people would think. I worried about what you would think when I was deployed. I worried about missing Kaylee and the distractions associated with loving someone. Loving both of you. I worried I wouldn't be able to do my job right. Bottom line, none of it made sense."

"And now?" he asked hesitantly.

Sierra shrugged. "I've seen the light, or you could say I've talked to the dog. We had a heart-to-heart on the way back to the base, and Rhaegar set me straight."

Noah felt relieved. "A talking dog? Will wonders never cease?" He grinned.

"Okay, so maybe I talked, and he listened. But then I listened to my heart. I thought a lot of things, all of them wrong. Everything I want and need is right here with you. I want it all. I know it sounds selfish, but I do. And I've figured out a way to get it—that is if you are still interested?" she asked, hope in her voice.

"Interested in what?" he teased.

"Me."

Noah's heart overflowed with joy hearing her admission. "After our kiss, do you have to ask about my intentions?"

"No, but I've been taught never to assume." Sierra's grin was the one he'd thought of so many times in the past weeks—half teasing, half-serious, but totally his.

"Assume away. I've missed you every single day and picked up the phone several times to try and convince you to see things differently. I can handle you in the military. I love all of you, and I will support you in any way possible. Just let us be a part of your life."

"I'm glad to hear that, Nurse Noah, because I love you, too. All of you." She laughed. "Just think of the free medical care..."

"Minx."

"Maybe, but you love me."

"That I do. So, what's next? What's your plan?"

Sierra let out a deep breath. "I didn't renew my military contract and I was able to buy out my leave days. All sixty of them. I didn't take vacation much— more like never. "I talked to Chad and confirmed the job offer at Whispering Pines was still open. I'm going to be working there and living in Hallbrook. I was hoping you'd see that as a good thing, and that maybe we could pick up where we left off."

"Or maybe not."

"What do you mean?" she asked, her voice laced with confusion.

"I don't want to pick up where we left off," Noah said, shaking his head.

"You don't?" Her brow was drawn tight.

"Nope. I want to fast-forward," he said, suddenly grinning to let her off the hook.

"How far forward?" She was catching on quick, her answering smile a relief.

Noah rose, made his way to the tree, and removed one of the ornaments held in place by a gold wire. Making his way back to her side, he dropped to one knee. "To the wedding part. Sierra Winters, will you agree to be my Mrs. Jackson. Forever and ever."

"*Dad*, I thought you—" Kaylee stopped, suddenly realizing what was going on. "Does this mean what I think it means?" she asked, hope and joy on her face as she danced her way toward them.

"I don't know. I'm waiting to hear Sierra's answer." Noah chuckled.

"Oops. I want to hear, too—ask her again. You've got to get it right."

Noah shook his head and laughed. "Sierra Winters, will you do me the honor of becoming my wife?"

Sierra's eyes had already filled with tears and were now overflowing. "Of course. I love you both with all of my heart but didn't dare dream this could come true."

"But you do now?" he asked hopefully.

"I do. I don't want to run away anymore. The only running I'm doing is toward you."

"Yay! There's going to be a wedding. And I'm going to be the flower girl. Right, Daddy?" she asked, jumping around and doing pirouettes.

"You will be the most beautiful flower girl ever." Noah looked back at Sierra. "What about the military? Aren't you going to miss that life?" He didn't want anything to come between them now or ever.

"No. I made the choice to leave on my own, so you wouldn't feel like I was doing it for you. I did it for me. I'll have the job with Chad, and I've switched my service over to the National Guard. One weekend a month is theirs. The rest of the time, I'm yours."

"I prefer to think of it as you're mine all of the time, and they're only borrowing you."

"I like the sound of that."

He rose, pulling Sierra into his arms, swinging her around in a circle.

"Do you have a ring, Daddy?" Kaylee asked.

"Well, this wasn't exactly planned, so this will have to do." Noah pulled the gold wire from his pocket and twisted it into a ring. "Until I can get you a real one."

"This is perfect," Sierra said as Noah slid the wire ring on her finger.

"This spot of the house really is magical." He leaned down to kiss his future bride.

Epilogue

ONE YEAR LATER...

Sierra was nervous. More than a little nervous. Now that the moment was upon her, and her son was about to make an entrance into the world, she was downright scared. It felt as though a whirlwind year had brought them to this point.

Noah had surprised her with an "official" engagement ring for Christmas and presented it in front of the whole family. He'd invited her parents, Tank and Camilla, and Laura and Kaylee. Everyone important in her life had been there to witness the moment.

She still wore the original wire ring on a chain around her neck. Call her sentimental, but to her, it was the real deal. The true symbol of the magic they'd shared when he dropped to one knee. Between him and Kaylee, she hadn't stood a chance of taking much time to organize the wedding. Her flower girl had insisted Valentine's Day was simply the most perfect wedding day.

Sierra had agreed.

Her mother and Laura had been all too happy to lend a hand to make it happen. The rest came naturally, but still far quicker than they'd thought—much to their joy.

But as nervous or scared as she was to become a mother, knowing an infant would be relying on her maternal instincts, her strength in facing the challenge came from God. And from knowing Noah was by her side every step of the way. Afterall, Noah was the experienced one.

"Are you ready?" the doctor asked. "It's almost time."

Noah took her hand and pulled it to his chest. "Let's do this," he said, dropping a kiss on her lips.

"We're ready," Sierra told the doctor. A sense of peace fell over her even as another contraction hit. This time, she embraced it instead of fighting it, knowing what was to come. She'd be able to hold her son in her arms for the first time. In honor of

Noah's father, Bradley Jackson was about to make his way into the world.

It was time to believe in herself. With Sierra's parents and her new family by her side, she'd make it work. Determination was no stranger in her life.

Fifteen crazy but joyful minutes later, the doctor placed a crying baby in her arms. "Congratulations, he's a healthy baby boy with an impressive set of pipes." The doctor smiled like this was the best part of his job.

The baby instantly settled down as if recognizing he was safe. "He's beautiful," she said, in awe of tiny baby she held.

"You both are," Noah added, his fingers gently tracing the baby's face and brushing back Sierra's hair. The love in his eyes was unmistakable.

"You'd better get Kaylee. She'll be going crazy out there."

"So true." He grinned, reluctantly letting go of her hand to go get his daughter. Their daughter. It was time for Kaylee to meet her brother. This past year had taught her it wasn't deeds that earned someone respect, it was love and honor.

Respect came from the heart.

What to Read Next...

Love & Joy
Book 8 of the Holidays in Hallbrook series – A
Sweet Easter Romance.
Let the battle begin...

If you enjoyed this sweet and charming romance,
be sure to check out the
ALSO BY ELSIE DAVIS section on the next page
for more clean and wholesome romance.

BONUS READ

Want to keep in touch with new releases and what's
happening in the world of Elsie Davis?

Sign up for the monthly newsletter at Elsie Davis HEA (Happily-Ever-After) and enjoy DIGGING THE DRIVER (A Celebrity Corgi Romance) as a FREE BOOK!

The greatest compliment you could give an author is to leave a review in order to help other readers discover the same great stories you enjoyed. Amazon/Bookbub/Goodreads are all great places. Many thanks!!!

Another great way to keep in touch - *Follow Elsie Davis on FaceBook*

Also By Elsie Davis

Sweet, Clean and Wholesome Stories...with a Happily-Ever-After Guarantee!

Holidays in Hallbrook
(Sweet Romance Series for Holidays Throughout the Year)
Welcome to Hallbrook, New Hampshire. A small-town filled with the unexpected, lots of love, and of course, a beloved dog to ramp up the excitement.
Love & Order (Labor Day)
Love & Family (Thanksgiving)
Love & Peace (Christmas)
Love & Chocolate (Valentine's Day)
Love & Hope (Mother's Day)
Love & Liberty (Independence Day)
Love & Honor (Veteran's Day)

Love & Joy (Easter)
Love & Adventure (Father's Day)

Great Smoky Mountain Getaways
(Christian Inspirational – Women's Fiction Ro-mances)
Juliet's Journey to Love
Poppy's Path to Love
Rachel's Road to Love

Crossroads Creek Cowboys
(Christian Inspirational Romances)
The Heart of a Cowboy
The Help of a Cowboy
The Return of a Cowboy
Coming Soon – The Care of a Cowboy

Crestfield Inn Romances
If you like special kinds of soulmates, a splash of
the supernatural, and wholesome relationships,

you'll adore this sweet bit of fun filled with romance and mystery.
Turning Back Time
Turning Up Roses
Turning Down Pie

Celebrity Corgi Romance
(Standalone Sweet Romance)
If you like light mystery mixed in with your happily-ever-after, you'll enjoy this second-chance
romance and the race to save an adorable Corgi.
Digging the Driver

Gold Coast Retrievers
(Sweet Romance)
***Special Golden Retrievers help their humans
solve mysteries, save lives, and even find love...***
Defending Dakota

Trinity River
(Sweet Western Romance)

Ranchers and farmers depend on the Trinity River for water, but when a secret conglomerate starts buying up property by fair means or foul, it's time for the landowners of Tumble County to fight back—Texas style. But what they don't count on, is finding love in the process.
Back in the Rancher's Arms
Small Town, Big Secrets

Coming Soon! (2023-2024)

Sundancer's Legacy – 9 Book series

Sundancer's Star
Sundancer's Joy
Sundancer's Heart
Sundancer's Majesty
Sundancer's Miracle
Sundancer's Glory
Sundancer's Kiss
Sundancer's Moon
Sundancer's Splendor

About The Author

Elsie Davis is a *USA Today and International Bestselling Author* of over 25 sweet, clean, and wholesome romances, and a member of the ACFW. She discovered the world of Happily-Ever-After romance at the age of twelve when she began avidly reading Barbara Cartland, the Queen of Romance, and has been hooked ever since. After building her dream log home on top of a small mountain, she turned her attention to do what she loves most, writing. Elsie writes sweet Contemporary Romance and Contemporary Christian Romance from her heart...hoping to share a little love in a big world.

When she's not writing, she can be found birding, kayaking, camping, fishing, playing disc golf, and taking nature walks—hoping to spot wildlife. Basically, she loves all things outdoors, EXCEPT cold weather. She and her husband are avid Caribbean cruisers, but Elsie's favorite vacation was their cruise to Alaska. (In spite of the cold!) Indoors, she enjoys a toasty fire, and of course, a great romance with a guaranteed Happily-Ever-After.

https://www.elsiedavishea.com